# ATTENT

Test your SF IQ alone, or compete with friends as you search for the answers to these and hundreds of other questions from the worlds of the extraterrestrial, the supernatural, and the just plain strange:

* What are close encounters of the first, second, and third kinds?

* On what planet did Isaac Asimov's Second Foundation reside?

* Tim O'Hara's uncle came from out of town. Where?

* What was the robot race that pursued the Ragtag Fleet in *Battlestar Galactica*?

* What was the only Ray Bradbury short story to appear as a *Twilight Zone* episode?

From the realms of TV, cinema, and literature come monsters and heroes, giants and robots, vampires and androids, aliens and sorcerers, and a host of other characters that inhabit the wonderful world of science fiction.

⊘ SIGNET BOOKS
(0451)

# FUN FOR THE WHOLE FAMILY

☐ **101 BEST MAGIC TRICKS by Guy Frederick.** Top magician Guy Frederick lets you into the inner circle of those who know what others never can even guess about how magic really works. Includes handkerchief tricks, card tricks, mind reading tricks, and much much more! (140109—$2.95)*

☐ **COLLECTING STAMPS by Paul Villard.** You'll find the answers to all your stamp collecting questions in this fascinating treasury of information. Everything you need to know to pursue the world's most popular hobby for fun, knowledge, and profit. (132211—$2.95)*

☐ **IN SEARCH OF TRIVIA by Jeff Rovin.** A great new collection of trivia questions guaranteed to challenge your mental prowess. 2400 brainbusters that cover books, celebrated couples, rock and roll, sports and more. (133137—$3.95)*

☐ **THE CALCULATOR GAME BOOK FOR KIDS OF ALL AGES by Arlene Hartman.** The essential handbook that presents hundreds of games, tricks, and puzzles for every age level and every grade level. (127080—$1.95)*

☐ **SCORE: BEATING THE TOP 16 VIDEO GAMES by Ken Uston.** The unique playing guide that shows you how to beat your favorite machine at its own game. (118138—$2.50)

*Prices slightly higher in Canada

---

Buy them at your local bookstore or use this convenient coupon for ordering.

**NEW AMERICAN LIBRARY**
P.O. Box 999, Bergenfield, New Jersey 07621

Please send me the books I have checked above. I am enclosing $＿＿＿＿
(please add $1.00 to this order to cover postage and handling). Send check or money order—no cash or C.O.D.'s. Prices and numbers are subject to change without notice.

Name ＿＿＿＿＿＿＿＿＿＿＿＿＿＿＿＿＿＿＿＿＿＿＿＿＿＿＿＿＿＿＿＿＿＿＿＿

Address ＿＿＿＿＿＿＿＿＿＿＿＿＿＿＿＿＿＿＿＿＿＿＿＿＿＿＿＿＿＿＿＿＿

City＿＿＿＿＿＿＿＿＿＿＿State＿＿＿＿＿＿＿＿Zip Code＿＿＿＿＿＿
Allow 4-6 weeks for delivery.
This offer is subject to withdrawal without notice.

# STARLOG
## SCIENCE FICTION
## TRIVIA
## BOOK

BY
**DAVID McDONNELL
JOHN SAYERS
&
TIM L. SMITH**

with additional questions by
**Eddie Berganza, Carr D'Angelo,
Robert Greenberger, David Hutchison
& Thomas F. Smith**

Illustrated by
**George Kochell**

A SIGNET BOOK

NEW AMERICAN LIBRARY

NAL BOOKS ARE AVAILABLE AT QUANTITY DISCOUNTS WHEN USED
TO PROMOTE PRODUCTS OR SERVICES. FOR INFORMATION PLEASE
WRITE TO PREMIUM MARKETING DIVISION, NEW AMERICAN LIBRARY,
1633 BROADWAY, NEW YORK, NEW YORK 10019.

Copyright © 1986 by Comics World Corp.

All rights reserved

Front cover photo credits:
"Spock," © 1982 Paramount Pictures
"E.T.," © 1982 Universal City Studios
"V," © 1984 Warner Bros. T.V.
"Darth Vader/Revenge of the Jedi," © 1982 Lucasfilm Ltd.
"Conan," © 1981 Dino DeLaurentis Corp.
"Harrison Ford/Raiders of the Lost Ark," © 1984 Lucasfilm Ltd.
"Superman," © 1983 D.C. Comics, Inc.
"Planet of The Apes," © 1968 20th Century Fox

SIGNET TRADEMARK REG. U.S. PAT. OFF. AND FOREIGN COUNTRIES
REGISTERED TRADEMARK—MARCA REGISTRADA
HECHO EN CHICAGO, U.S.A.

SIGNET, SIGNET CLASSIC, MENTOR, ONYX, PLUME, MERIDIAN AND NAL BOOKS
are published by New American Library,
1633 Broadway, New York, New York 10019

First Signet Printing, September, 1986

1  2  3  4  5  6  7  8  9

PRINTED IN THE UNITED STATES OF AMERICA

# Contents

## QUESTIONS:

Cult Culture ———————————————— 7
Today's Genre ———————————————— 10
Heroes & Heroines ——————————————— 13
I, Robot ——————————————————— 18
Fantasy Geography ——————————————— 21
Quotes ————————————————————— 24
Boo! Hiss! (Villains) —————————————— 26
ALiens & Other BEMs ————————————— 32
Epic Fiction ————————————————— 34
Special Effects ————————————————— 37
Star Trek —————————————————— 40
Teen Fantasies &
   Amazing Stuff ———————————————— 45
Ecology ———————————————————— 48
Bizarre Stuff ————————————————— 51
Sword & Sorcery ————————————————— 54
Star Wars —————————————————— 57
Irwin Allen Fun ————————————————— 62
Apes & Primates ————————————————— 65
SF Women ——————————————————— 68
The Doctor ————————————————— 70
Funny Stuff ————————————————— 74
Battlestar Galactica ——————————————— 77
Oscars & Honors ————————————————— 80
The Written Word ————————————————— 83
Twilight Zone ————————————————— 89
Classics ————————————————————— 92
Songs & Sounds ————————————————— 95
Animations of Life ——————————————— 98
SF TV ——————————————————— 103
Wondrous Worlds ————————————————— 106
Giant or Otherwise Unusual Animals ——————— 109
See You in the Funny Papers ————————— 111
"V"—The Saga ————————————————— 116
Buck & Flash ————————————————— 118
The Bloody Pulps ———————————————— 121

Time Travel & Odysseys Two _____ 124
Utopias & Distopias_____ 127
Missions _____ 130
Runners, Rebels, & Replicants _____ 133
Heavens Above, Hells Below _____ 136
Spies & Intrigue _____ 139
Scary Stuff _____ 142
Legends & Myths _____ 144
Tarzans _____ 147
Truly Bad Sci-Fi _____ 150
The End of the World _____ 153
The Answers _____ 156
Trivia Photo Answers _____ 207

# Cult Culture

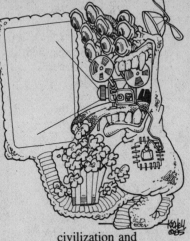

CC-1: Who coined the term "sci-fi?"

CC-2: Where did the Body Snatchers invade?

CC-3: What was Steve McQueen's *first* film?

CC-4: Name the movie *J.R.* shot.

CC-5: Who played *The Man Who Fell to Earth* in the movies?

CC-6: What anti-gravity material was invented by Fred MacMurray in *The Absent-Minded Professor*?

CC-7: Where did Professor Rotwang toil?

CC-8: And where did most of the action of *Dawn of the Dead* take place?

CC-9: With what death ray did the evil scientist Durand Durand threaten civilization and Barbarella?

CC-10: Upon what did *The Abominable Dr. Phibes* base his murders?

CC-11: What did Alex call his buddies in *A Clockwork Orange*?

CC-12: Who was the *Stranger in a Strange Land*?

CC-13: What did the Emotional Stimulator Machine do to Barbarella?

CC-14: Name the characters portrayed by Tony Randall in

*The Seven Faces of Dr. Lao.*

CC-15: What film spawned the 3-D rage in the 1950s?

CC-16: What was the object of *Death Race 2000*?

CC-17: Where was *Night of the Living Dead* filmed?

CC-18: What film is *Poltergeist* director Tobe Hooper renowned for?

CC-19: *The Man with X-Ray Eyes* was . . . ?

CC-20: Name the two sequels to 1958's *The Fly*?

CC-21: What is the most precious commodity in the world of *The Road Warrior*?

CC-22: What actor appeared in *The Blues Brothers, The Empire Strikes Back, An American Werewolf in London* and *Trading Places*?

CC-23: What was the name of Mork's superior?

CC-24: Who directed *The Fearless Vampire Killers*? The female lead was

HOLLYWOOD BOULEVARD PHOTO: COPYRIGHT © 1976 NEW WORLD PICTURES

his wife. Name
her, too.

CC-25: What are close
encounters of the
first, second,

and third kinds?
And have *you*
had any?

*(Answers appear on page 156)*

**What two genre legends are toasting each other on (and in)**
***Hollywood Boulevard*?**

# Today's Genre

TG-1: What was unusual about the casting of Jimmy Hunt in Tobe Hooper's remake of *Invaders from Mars*?

TG-2: How many years was Ripley in sleep hibernation between the events of *ALIEN* and its sequel, *ALIENS*?

TG-3: Who created *Howard the Duck*?

TG-4: The robots of the *Cherry 2000* series have many uses. Sam Treadwell seems most interested in one of them. What's that?

TG-5: Who leads *The Misfits of Science*?

TG-6: In *Project X*, Matthew Broderick's extremely intelligent friend is named Virgil. What's unusual about him?

TG-7: After several years' absence, what two actresses return to the world of *Star Trek* in *Star Trek IV*? And what are their relationships to *Trek* personnel?

TG-8: Who voices the nasty rat who's the enemy of *The Great Mouse Detective*?

TG-9: He says "I'm alive" a lot. Who is he?

TG-10: What's the best, the only—and a very messy—way to kill an Immortal, according to *Highlander* mythos?

TG-11: Terry Jones scripted the Jim Henson–George Lucas collaboration of *Labyrinth*. For what is Jones best known?

TG-12: In what 1985 film (*not* science fiction!) did special FX master Ray Harryhausen make a cameo appearance?

BIG TROUBLE IN LITTLE CHINA PHOTO: JOHN SHANNON/COPYRIGHT © 1986 20TH CENTURY FOX

**Jack Burton (Kurt Russell) is in *Big Trouble in Little China*. Just what is Burton's profession? And as to Russell, how many movies has he made with director John Carpenter?**

TG-13: With the late Rod Serling obviously unavailable as the omniscient narrator of *The Twilight Zone*, to whom did the producers of the revived series turn? In what episode(s) of the original series did this actor appear?

TG-14: Don Johnson and Glenn Frey appear in a Pepsi commercial. What noted genre director helmed the ad?

TG-15: Twelve-year-old David Freeman leaves home one day in 1978. He returns—not aged one day—only to find it is now 1986. What movie storyline is he experiencing?

TG-16: Can *The Boy Who Could Fly* do so?

TG-17: In *Labyrinth*, who portrays the heroine? And what actor is seen as the feared Goblin King?

TG-18: If you were traipsing through the Room of Upside-Down Hell or wading through the River of Ashes with Jack Burton and Gracie Law, where would you be?

TG-19: Director Jim Cameron and stars Michael Biehn and Lance Henriksen were reunited for *ALIENS*. On what previous unexpected success did they toil?

TG-20: What face lurks beneath the satanic visage of *Legend*'s Darkness?

TG-21: It involves Dino De Laurentiis, heart transplants, and giant animals. What sequel is it?

TG-22: Problems with matter transmission crop up once again in David Cronenberg's remake of *The Fly*. But what's the major difference in how the experiment's effects manifest themselves in Jeff Goldblum, Cronenberg's *Fly* scientist?

TG-23: What comedy superstar confronts Oriental mysticism and magical monsters (devised by Richard Edlund's FX team) to rescue *The Golden Child*?

TG-24: In the world of *Legend*, what happens when you kill off unicorns?

TG-25: Teen boy finds love with alien girl. OK, so it has happened before, but in what recent film (which also starred Keenan Wynn)?

*(Answers appear on pages 157–58)*

# Heroes & Heroines

**HH-1:** What two actors portrayed Captain Video?

**HH-2:** What did Carl Kolchak do for a living and what was his hobby?

**HH-3:** Name Germany's most popular science-fiction hero.

**HH-4:** Name the characters played by Martin Landau and Barbara Bain in *Space: 1999*.

**HH-5:** Who is Colonel Steve Austin?

**HH-6:** Who is Colonel Steve Trevor?

**HH-7:** Who is Arthur Dent?

**HH-8:** What was *The Prisoner*'s real name?

**HH-9:** Jose Ferrer, Chuck Connors, Herbert Lom and James Mason. What role did they all play?

**HH-10:** What late actor played *The Immortal*?

**HH-11:** *The Absent-Minded Professor,* in his earlier acting days, was used as the model for what comic-book character?

**HH-12:** Who were the Solid Six of James Michener's epic novel *Space*?

**HH-13:** Exactly what was *TRON*?

HH-14: How did TV's *Mr. Terrific* get so terrific?

HH-15: Who was *The Last Starfighter*?

HH-16: Venkman, Stantz, Spengler and Zeddmore are a group of professionals. Professional what?

HH-17: Who recently had a fowl 50th birthday?

HH-18: Michael Crawford stars as Woody Wilkins in what Disney superheroic adventure?

HH-19: Patrick Hale is a World Television Network reporter in what film?

HH-20: Who served as *Rocky Jones, Space Ranger*?

HH-21: And what author created Professor Bernard Quatermass?

HH-22: Atom, Midnight and Zero all share what rank in common?

**Superman (Christopher Reeve) isn't getting married, but he *is* appearing in a soap opera. Which one?**

LOVE OF LIFE PHOTO: COURTESY CBS

HH-23: Who was the main partner of agent James West in *The Wild Wild West*?

HH-24: What do Ralph Byrd, Morgan Conway and Warren Beatty have in common?

HH-25: Brian Donlevy, Andrew Keir and John Mills have what *film* role in common?

HH-26: Who gave Steven Spielberg the look for Indiana Jones' outfit?

HH-27: Tom Corbett was a space cadet at Space Academy. What was he training to become?

HH-28: What was the name of Harry Harrison's Stainless Steel Rat?

HH-29: Name the detective in Asimov's *The Caves of Steel*, *The Naked Sun* and *The Robots of Dawn*.

HH-30: Who did George C. Scott think he was in *They Might Be Giants*? And who was Joanne Woodward?

**Name the plane that Jake (Stephen Collins) flew during *Tales of the Gold Monkey*.**

GOLD MONKEY PHOTO: ABC

HH-31: Who created Professor Challenger?

HH-32: What was unusual about the physical appearance of *The Man from Atlantis*?

HH-33: Who was Indiana Jones named for?

HH-34: Jane Fonda toured the stars, spreading love, in which film?

HH-35: Who was Karen Allen in the movie *Starman*?

HH-36: Upon what novel was *The Six Million Dollar Man* based?

HH-37: And what does OSI stand for?

HH-38: Who was a companion to *The Invisible Boy*?

HH-39: In 1964, who conquered the Martians?

**These folks look as lucky as lucky can be. The song they've just wrapped is?**

MARY POPPINS PHOTO: COPYRIGHT © 1982 WALT DISNEY PRODUCTIONS

HH-40: Who hit a golf ball on the Moon?

HH-41: What American actor appeared in *Godzilla*? And again in *Godzilla 1985*?

HH-42: Name the actors who have portrayed *Doctor Who*.

HH-43: In what film does a love affair take place between a man of the Rock Tribe and a woman of the Shell People?

HH-44: Who is Linda Lee Danvers' famous cousin?

HH-45: Kato was this masked man's sidekick. Who was he?

HH-46: The Lady of the Lake presented this gift. What was it and who received it?

HH-47: In *Blade Runner*, how long did Rachael have to live?

HH-48: Name *Mad Max*'s late son.

HH-49: Who is Steve Rogers?

HH-50: Who is Anthony Rogers?

*(Answers appear on pages 158–59)*

# I, Robot

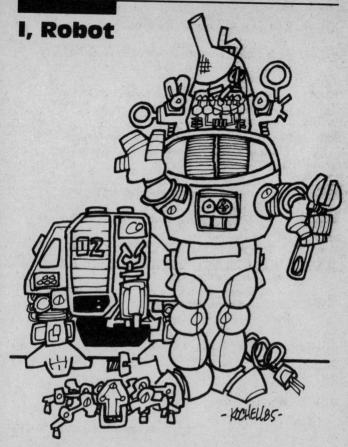

— KOCHELL85 —

R-1: What was the name of the robot maid of TV's *The Jetsons*?

R-2: Who was the robot maid's boy friend on *The Jetsons*?

R-3: Who was *My Living Doll*?

R-4: In *Colossus: The Forbin Project*, what was the Soviet counterpart to Colossus?

R-5:   Who was the voice of the Proteus IV computer?

R-6:   What are the Three Laws of Robotics?

R-7:   Who set forth the Three Laws of Robotics?

R-8:   The voice of KITT on NBC's *Knight Rider* is furnished by what actor?

R-9:   Who created *The Six Million Dollar Man*?

R-10:  What game does Matthew Broderick play with the computer in *WarGames*?

R-11:  In what film does Klaus Kinski create Don Opper and Kendra Kirchner?

R-12:  Identify Aqua-Com and Val-Com.

R-13:  The robot of Oz is . . . ?

R-14:  What did Dr. Rotwang create in Fritz Lang's *Metropolis*?

R-15:  Name the three books in D. F. Jones' Colossus trilogy.

R-16:  What android was left emotionally incomplete by his creator, Emil Vaslovik?

R-17:  Who played Hymie the Robot on *Get Smart*?

R-18:  Who coined the term "robot"?

R-19:  How is the robot in *Saturn 3* destroyed?

R-20:  Who was the voice of *The Colossus of New York*? Exactly what was this Colossus?

R-21:  What was unique about the robot in *3-D Robot Monster*?

R-22:  *Holmes and Yoyo*. Which one was the robot, and who played him?

R-23: Who was "The World's Mightiest Robot," controlled by 12-year-old Jimmy Sparks?

R-24: And who is the manufacturer of magical dolls in the opera *Tales of Hoffman?*

R-25: In *Creation of the Humanoids,* what was the derogatory term for robots?

*(Answers appear on pages 159–60)*

**This "first" robot (seen in *The Outer Limits*) was created in short stories by Eando Binder. Who is he?**

OUTER LIMITS PHOTO: COURTESY ABC

# Fantasy Geography

FG-1: What would you find if you moved to Stepford, Connecticut?

FG-2: To what planet was Billy Pilgrim taken and displayed in *Slaughterhouse-Five*?

FG-3: Where would you find Clay Men, Lion Men and Hawk Men?

FG-4: Where do the Martians first land in Orson Welles' *War of the Worlds*?

FG-5: What planet is the home of Asimov's Foundation?

FG-6: Name the four *original* areas of Disneyland.

FG-7: Where is Pellucidar?

FG-8: On what two islands does the action of *King Kong* take place?

FG-9: In what country does Indiana Jones find the Temple of Doom?

FG-10: Where did Puff the Magic Dragon live?

FG-11: Where does Little Nemo spend his every non-waking moment?

FG-12: In *Out of the Silent Planet*, name the silent planet.

FG-13: In the C.S. Lewis space series, what are Venus, Mars and Jupiter called by their inhabitants?

FG-14: On what planet did Isaac Asimov's Second Foundation reside?

FG-15: Name the bowl-shaped world in Hal Clement's *Mission of Gravity* (1954).

FG-16: Name the *Deathworld* in Harry Harrison's novel (1960).

FG-17: Where does Paul Maud'Dib Atreides rule?

FG-18: If you were a Red or Black Lectroid and wanted to go home for the holidays, where would you go?

**Where do cowboys and dinosaurs roam?**

VALLEY OF GWANGI PHOTO: COPYRIGHT © 1969 WARNER BROS. SEVEN ARTS, INC.

FG-19: What landmark served as the rendezvous point for aliens and humans in *Close Encounters of the Third Kind*?

FG-20: Where is *Saturn 3* set?

FG-21: Name the giant, cylindrical artificial world created by Arthur C. Clarke.

FG-22: On what planet did the action of *Barbarella* occur?

FG-23: Where is Richard Cowper's novel *Profundis* set?

FG-24: In what city was the spaceship discovered in *Five Million Years to Earth*?

FG-25: On what planet does the race of Fuzzies dwell?

*(Answers appear on pages 160–61)*

# Quotes

For most of these quotations, you must identify the source (speaker and film/TV/book).

Q-1: "All the universe—or nothingness. Which shall it be?"

Q-2: "All these worlds are yours except Europa. Attempt no landings there."

Q-3: "Where are we going?" "Planet 10!" "When?" "Real soon!"

Q-4: "You may strike me down, but I'll come back more powerful than even you can imagine."

Q-5: ". . . 'twas beauty killed the beast."

Q-6: "We belong to the dead."

Q-7: "Danger Will Robinson! Warning!"

Q-8: "I'm a doctor, not a mechanic!"

Q-9: "So long, and thanks for all the fish."

Q-10: "There is nothing wrong with your television set."

Q-11: "You don't usually see that kind of behavior in a major appliance."

Q-12: "I will not be pushed, filed, stamped, in-dexed, briefed, debriefed, or numbered."

Q-13: "To God, there is no zero. I still exist."

Q-14: "No job is too great for Duck

Dodgers in the 24th-and-a-half Century!''

Q-15: "All the world will be your enemy, (Prince with a Thousand Enemies), and whenever they catch you, they will kill you. But first they must catch you."

Q-16: "Open the pod bay doors, Hal."

Q-17: "No bucks, no Buck Rogers."

Q-18: "I, Anthony Rogers, am, so far as I know, the only man alive whose normal span of life has been spread over a period of 573 years."

Q-19: "All this happened, more or less."

Q-20: "Love means never having to say you're ugly" was the keynote of the advertising campaign of what popular genre film?

Q-21: What words did Patricia Neal say to Gort to stop the destruction of the Earth?

Q-22: 'Yes, Commissioner.''

Q-23: "The weed of crime bears bitter fruit. Crime does not pay."

Q-24: "I have a feeling you were put here for a reason."

Q-25: "Shocking."

*(Answers appear on pages 161–62)*

**He may be wearing a towel, but Spock addresses another subject when he remembers his "death" in this scene from *Star Trek III*. What does he say?**

STAR TREK III PHOTO: COPYRIGHT © 1984 PARAMOUNT PICTURES

# Boo! Hiss! (Villains)

BH-1: Boris Karloff was originally slated to play this role. Instead, it went to Claude Rains. Name the movie.

BH-2: Abbott and Costello met the Invisible Man briefly in 1948. Who supplied his voice?

BH-3: Who created Dr. Fu Manchu?

BH-4: How many Hitler clones survived in *The Boys From Brazil*?

BH-5: When Boris Karloff was Gruesome, whom did he meet?

BH-6: Who did Mr. Schubert menace? And who played Schubert?

BH-7: Name the men who have portrayed Ernst Stavro Blofeld on screen.

BH-8: "Riddle me this: who played me in the *Batman* TV series? Hooohoohaa ha haaaaa!"

BH-9: What character created the Daleks?

BH-10: Who were the two races of aliens in *Buckaroo Banzai*? Where were they from?

BH-11: What does Diana do to bunnies in "*V*"?

BH-12: Name a role played by Kirk Douglas, Boris Karloff and Jack Palance.

BH-13: In the TV series *Fantastic Journey*, who was cast in the "Dr. Smith"-type role?

BH-14: What planet does Darkseid rule?

BH-15: Who was the voice of Lucifer on *Battlestar Galactica*?

BH-16: What was the robot race which pursued the humans in *Battlestar Galactica*?

BH-17: Who portrayed John Bigbooté, Commander Kruge, Butch Cavendish and the Reverend Jim?

BH-18: Who is the traitor of *Dune*?

BH-19: Who has portrayed Jack the Ripper, the Evil Genius, Dr. Necessiter, and that really diabolical computer program Sark?

BH-20: In what film might Revok blow you up real good?

BH-21: What was the name of the robot in *Saturn 3*?

BH-22: Name the large, nasty robot in Disney's *The Black Hole*.

BH-23: Name the actor who was Ming the Merciless, the Exorcist and the enemy of Doug and Bob McKenzie.

**He may be merciless but he has good taste in women. Who is this Ming?**

FLASH GORDON PHOTO: UNIVERSAL

**MONSTER FROM HELL PHOTO: COPYRIGHT © 1973 HAMMER FILMS**

**He's once again behind the mask in *Frankenstein and the Monster from Hell*. Who is he?**

BH-24: Name the actors who have portrayed the Phantom of the Opera on *film*.

BH-25: Who portrayed the famous fiend Dr. Miguelito Loveless, and where did he appear?

BH-26: Why did Dr. Doom originally wear a mask?

BH-27: Who was the plan-upsetting mutant in Asimov's *Foundation and Empire*?

BH-28: Nargola, Mook the Moon Man, Kul of Eos, Heng Foo Seeng and Dr. Clysmok all fought what SF hero?

BH-29: Name the arch-enemy of *Jason of Star Command*.

BH-30: Who was Sark's boss in *TRON*?

BH-31: What actor menaced the first James Bond on television?

BH-32: What is the preferred meal for much of the cast of *Night of the Living Dead*?

BH-33: What was most everyone trying to do to sweet Charlotte in *Hush, Hush, Sweet Charlotte*?

BH-34: How do the two monsters "die" when *Frankenstein Meets the Wolf Man*?

BH-35: Why does *Nyah, Devil Girl from Mars*, come to Scotland in the 1954 movie?

BH-36: How tall is the woman in *Attack of the 50-Foot Woman*?

BH-37: SPECTRE stands for . . . ?

BH-38: Who was Glenn Strange?

BH-39: Dr. Strangelove and company learned to love what?

BH-40: *Gremlins* had their own version of the Wicked Witch. Who was she?

BH-41: Who is the Queen of Bartertown?

BH-42: Modred is her son. Arthur is her brother. Evil is her game. What is her name?

BH-43: Who foils the dastardly plots of both the Professor and the Master Cylinder with the help of a supernatural satchel?

BH-44: Snidely Whiplash menaced who?

BH-45: What is Ray Bradbury referring to when he states that *Something Wicked This Way Comes*?

BH-46: Simon (Barsinister) sez, who am I?

BH-47: Joan Collins had a song of death for this TV crime fighter. Who was she and whom did she croon for?

BH-48: What is similar about the antagonists of *Splash* and *Starman*?

BH-49: Who does Shang-Chi, Master of Kung Fu, pay his disrespect to on Father's Day?

BH-50: First, he menaced Maxwell Smart and then he menaced passengers on the Looooove Boat, who is he?

*(Answers appear on pages 162–64)*

# Aliens & Other BEMs

**A-1:** What was the name of the cat in *ALIEN*?

**A-2:** Name the *ALIEN* writer who acts in *Dark Star*.

**A-3:** Upon what part of the body does an inhabitant of Ork sit?

**A-4:** Name *My Favorite Martian*.

**A-5:** Who suggested that *Martians, Go Home*?

**A-6:** What do *Uforia*, *ALIEN* and *Christine* have in common?

**A-7:** In the original screenplay (and the novelization), what does E.T. like to eat?

**A-8:** Veronica (*ALIEN*) Cartwright's sister starred in what two popular TV series?

**A-9:** Tim O'Hara's uncle came from out of town. Where?

**A-10:** Where does *The Brother from Another Planet* crash land on Earth?

**A-11:** Who designed the *ALIEN*?

**A-12:** In the film *Q*, what does Q stand for?

**A-13:** What shouldn't you do around a pod in *Invasion of the Body Snatchers*?

**A-14:** The *Invaders from Mars* were all what?

A-15: Manly Wade Wellman and his son collaborated on a Sherlock Holmes story. In this tale, Holmes and Watson face the invasion of Earth by what?

A-16: What was the major way you could distinguish one of TV's *Invaders* from an Earthling?

A-17: What destroyed the invading Martians in *War of the Worlds*?

A-18: What was the menace in *Forbidden Planet*?

A-19: Who directed *Dark Star*?

A-20: BEM. What does it mean?

A-21: What radio repertory group scared America with an alien invasion?

A-22: What extraterrestrial battled Quake in the Quaker Oats cereal wars in the '70s?

A-23: What agency fought to protect Japan from the onslaught of countless monsters?

A-24: Where were *The Mysterions* from?

A-25: Earth's monsters often defend the planet from alien invaders. And where do many of them (and Godzilla) reside?

*(Answers appear on pages 164–65)*

**Which *Zombie from the Stratosphere* went on where no man has gone before?**

PHOTO: REPUBLIC PICTURES CORPORATION

# Epic Fiction

EF-1: In what series will you find the adventures of Mark Twain, Sir Richard Burton, Jesus Christ and Tom Mix?

EF-2: What day is Bilbo and Frodo Baggins' birthday?

EF-3: Who created Tom Swift?

EF-4: What are the four families whose sagas make up James Michener's epic novel *Space*?

EF-5: Who perfected the science of psychohistory?

EF-6: Name the members of the Fellowship of the Ring.

EF-7: Name the four books of Isaac Asimov's Foundation series.

EF-8: How many Farthings make up The Shire?

EF-9: From what earthly affliction did Thomas Covenant the Unbeliever suffer?

EF-10: What was the official title of the leader of Asimov's Second Foundation?

EF-11: What age of Middle Earth is the setting of *The Lord of the Rings*?

EF-12: What was the name of Mark Twain's first river-boat in the Farmer series?

EF-13: Who is King Theoden's door-warden?

EF-14: What is Edgar Rice Burroughs' name for Mars?

EF-15: How many Nazgul (Black Riders) were there?

EF-16: In what country was J.R.R. Tolkien born?

EF-17: Who wrote *The Worm Ouroboros*?

EF-18: Where might one find Old Man Willow?

**How long did it take on film to go *Around the World in 80 Days*?**

AROUND THE WORLD PHOTO: COPYRIGHT © 1956 UNITED ARTISTS

EF-19: For whom was the role of Wizard in MGM's *The Wizard of Oz* originally written?

EF-20: Who created Mary Poppins?

EF-21: Katherine Kurtz is best known for her fantasy novels set on what alternative worlds?

EF-22: What is Conan's native land?

EF-23: Where does Thomas Covenant find himself— much to his displeasure?

EF-24: What is the large counterpart of Lilliput in *Gulliver's Travels*?

EF-25: King Kull ruled what island country?

*(Answers appear on pages 165–66)*

# Special Effects

**FX-1:** How many animated skeletons battle Jason and his crew at the end of Ray Harryhausen's *Jason and the Argonauts*?

**FX-2:** What was the special front projection process used to make Superman fly?

**FX-3:** What color is Darth Vader's light saber?

**FX-4:** What special effects process debuted in *Outland*?

**FX-5:** Willis O'Brien brought what famous fantasy character to life?

**FX-6:** Name three films which had effects shot in 65mm.

**FX-7:** Who were the four effects supervisors for *2001*?

**FX-8:** Name Ray Harryhausen's first color feature.

**FX-9:** Who animated the Id monster in *Forbidden Planet*?

**FX-10:** In what Technicolor classic can

the set for the great wall in *King Kong* be seen engulfed in flames?

FX-11: Holograms were first used in what feature film?

FX-12: Effects supervisor David Horsley instructed Technicolor to print in false colors for a transformation sequence in what classic SF film?

FX-13: How many fingers did George Pal's Martians have when they visited in *War of the Worlds*?

FX-14: Name three films with special-effects-created tornadoes.

FX-15: What film had a computer named "Mother?"

FX-16: What Jules Verne story was filmed in Todd-AO?

FX-17: What SF film was the first to feature aliens in *color*?

FX-18: Who played the title character in *The Thing from Another World*?

FX-19: What was the first film to feature the destruction of the entire world in glorious Technicolor?

FX-20: What special effects process allowed Carl Sagan to stroll through the ancient library of Alexandria in *Cosmos*?

FX-21: Name two movies released in Sensurround.

FX-22: What movie holds the world's record for the longest makeup application to a single actor?

FX-23: What *SF* film holds the record for the world's largest indoor set?

FX-24: Before the Academy of Motion Picture Arts and Science made makeup a regular category for Oscars in 1981, two special Oscars were awarded for outstanding makeup for science fiction/fantasy films. What were the films? Who received the Oscars?

FX-25: Name three theatrical films after *Forbidden Planet* in which Robby the Robot appeared.

*(Answers appear on pages 166–67)*

# Star Trek

ST-1: What can a phaser do?

ST-2: What Frederic Brown short story was adapted as an episode of *Star Trek*?

ST-3: What is the serial number of the shuttlecraft of the *U.S.S. Enterprise*? And the name of the craft?

ST-4: What is Harry Mudd's full name?

ST-5: Who wrote "The Trouble with Tribbles" episode of *Star Trek*?

ST-6: In what film did Leonard Nimoy *first* play an alien?

ST-7: Who is the only actor to have played members of three races—Romulan, Vulcan, and Klingon—in the *Star Trek* saga?

ST-8: Does Spock have a first name?

ST-9: In how many episodes of *Star Trek* did the *U.S.S. Enterprise* visit 20th Century Earth?

ST-10: In *Star Trek*, how did Khan escape from the 20th Century?

ST-11: Where is Dr. Leonard "Bones" McCoy from?

ST-12: What do the colors of the shirts worn by Starfleet crew on TV's *Star Trek* signify?

ST-13: What two actresses have essayed the role of Saavik?

ST-14: How often do Vulcans experience Pon Farr?

ST-15: What tune did Scott play at the memorial service of Captain Spock? And on what?

ST-16: Who commanded the *U.S.S. Enterprise* before James T. Kirk?

ST-17: Which author gave Spock a son—and in what *Trek* project?

ST-18: What color is Spock's blood?

ST-19: What is the name of the standard Romulan spaceship?

ST-20: Where is rank indicated on a Starfleet uniform (TV series)?

**What is so strange about this couple?**

ST-21: In what Texas city can you find Star Trek Lane?

ST-22: What powers phasers, tricorders and warp engines?

ST-23: Who are Sarek and Amanda?

ST-24: In how many live-action *Treks* did Harry Mudd appear?

ST-25: During its first season, where was *Star Trek* aired?

ST-26: In the *MAD* magazine parody of *Star Trek*, what was the name of the starship?

ST-27: Who built a web around the *U.S.S. Enterprise*?

ST-28: What actor portrayed Harry Mudd?

ST-29: The author of *Psycho* wrote three scripts for *Star Trek*. Name him and them.

ST-30: What world inhabited by super beings imposed a peace treaty on the Federation and the Klingon Empire?

ST-31: Name the two regular characters added to the animated *Star Trek* series.

STAR TREK PHOTO; COPYRIGHT PARAMOUNT PICTURES TELEVISION

ST-32: Like Spock, Saavik is a half-breed. Spock is half-Vulcan, half-human. What is Saavik's heritage?

ST-33: Which academy training exercise did James Kirk win by changing the rules?

ST-34: Cyrano Jones sold what?

ST-35: Which actor was not represented on the animated series but wrote an episode?

ST-36: Which writers contributed scripts to both TV and animated episodes?

ST-37: Which writers contributed to live-action and/or animated episodes and novels?

ST-38: In what episodes did *Dynasty* stars appear? Who were they it?

ST-39: Where are the impulse engines located on the *Enterprise*?

ST-40: In the *Saturday Night Live* spoof of *Star Trek*, which regulars portrayed Kirk, Spock, McCoy and Scotty?

ST-41: How many comic book versions of *Star Trek* have there been? By whom?

ST-42: Besides *Star Trek: The Motion Picture*, what other major SF films did Robert Wise direct?

ST-43: Who is T'Pring?

ST-44: An episode introduced a character who was slated for his own series, who was it?

ST-45: What is the *Enterprise* armed with?

ST-46: *Star Trek: The Motion Picture*'s plot is similar to which two TV episodes?

**ST-47:** According to Vonda McIntyre's novelization of *Star Trek III: The Search for Spock*, are Kruge and the Klingon spy, Valkris, lovers?

**ST-48:** What *Tootsie* star appeared on the TV *Trek*? What was her role?

**ST-49:** What important fact about Peter Preston was edited out of the theatrical release of *The Wrath of Khan*?

**ST-50:** She was Mrs. Danvers in Alfred Hitchcock's *Rebecca*, who was she in *The Search for Spock*?

*(Answers appear on pages 167–69)*

When Dame Judith Anderson first came on the set of *Star Trek III*, with what song was she serenaded by cast and crew?

STAR TREK III PHOTO: JOHN SHANNON/COPYRIGHT © 1984 PARAMOUNT PICTURES

# Teen Fantasies & Amazing Stuff

TF-1: Define D.A.R.Y.L.

TF-2: If you were in a 1985 teen SFX comedy and you battled a Tyrannosaurus Rex, just where would you be?

TF-3: To what year does Marty McFly return to meet his young parents-to-be-maybe?

TF-4: The teen heroes of *Real Genius* employed a unique method to prepare one of America's favorite movie snacks. What did they do?

TF-5: Name the aliens discovered by the young *Explorers*.

TF-6: She's cute. She's sweet. She's played by Raquel Welch's actress daughter, Tahnee. But what is she?

TF-7: What famed Earth cultural hero does Jeriba Shigan insult during the events of *Enemy Mine*?

TF-8: If you left before the credits of *Young Sherlock Holmes* ended, what important "fact" would you have missed?

TF-9: What three actresses had cameos in the initial episode of *Amazing Stories*? And what are their relationships to the segment's director?

TF-10: Because of an unfortunate typo in the world of *Brazil*, Tuttle became Buttle, causing the innocent Buttle to be arrested and terminated. Who was Tuttle?

TF-11: Which '60s group provides the new musical theme for the revived *Twilight Zone*?

TF-12: And who composed the main musical theme for *Amazing Stories*?

TF-13: OK, what was so amazing about Steven Spielberg's "The Mission"?

TF-14: Quentin Crisp assisted at the creation of what recent "monster"?

TF-15: The teen heroes of *Weird Science* got their idea to create the perfect woman from what classic film? (And it *isn't* the one you might think!)

TF-16: Who played the 19-year-old nymphomaniac trying to help Dr. Wolper regrow his dead wife?

TF-17: Which of the *Explorers* named their craft the *Thunder Road*?

TF-18: What color is Michael J. Fox's underwear when he first finds himself in the past before going *Back to the Future*?

TF-19: Its director described it as "Walter Mitty meets Franz Kafka." What was the movie's final title?

TF-20: Writer/director John Sayles adapted a bestselling book for the screen (though he didn't direct it). He had an alternate title for the movie, *Roots: The Early Years*. By what is it better known?

TF-21: William Katt and Sean Young adopted a dinosaur infant dubbed *Baby*. What species of heretofore-considered-extinct dinosaur is Baby?

TF-22: Space vampires are discovered in a craft hidden in Halley's Comet. When they arrive on Earth, what is it they want to rob humanity of?

TF-23: Name *The Goonies*.

TF-24: Whose FX facility provided the creatures for the Wonderland of *Dream Child*?

TF-25: Roddy McDowall's fearful horror TV host was named in tribute to two genre actors. Who are the pair saluted in *Fright Night*?

*(Answers appear on pages 169–70)*

**He's Mr. Alien Entertainment, Wak (Bob Picardo), yocking it up with *Explorers*. But what other creatures-in-makeup has he portrayed for makeup master Rob Bottin and director Joe Dante?**

EXPLORERS PHOTO: COPYRIGHT © 1985 PARAMOUNT PICTURES CORPORATION

# Ecology

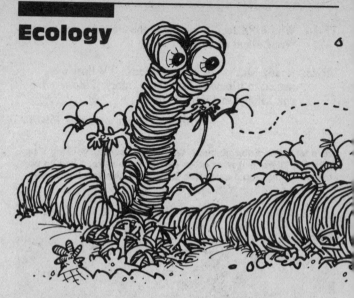

E-1: What was Soylent Green?

E-2: What was the name of the space freighter in *Silent Running* and its lone crewman? What was its cargo?

E-3: What was taking its revenge on Ray Milland and his family in a 1972 film?

E-4: In Jeannot Szwarc's *Bug*, what are the monsters and where do they come from?

E-5: What happens to the Earth in *The Day the Earth Caught Fire* (besides catching fire)?

E-6: Who is the antagonist in Roger Corman's *Little Shop of Horrors*?

E-7: What film mixes cattle mutilations, Watergate paranoia and nerve gas experiments?

E-8: Burt Lancaster and Charles Laughton. What medical role did they share?

E-9: What killed the Triffids?

E-10: If you were the Mummy, what would your favorite food be?

E-11: In *Invasion of the Bee Girls* (1973), what happens to Earth's housewives?

E-12: He was nicknamed "The Gill Man," but what was he better known as?

E-13: John Brunner's *Stand on Zanzibar* is concerned with the dangers of what?

E-14: What company mines Io in *Outland*?

E-15: What happened to Colonel Glen Manning after he was exposed to radiation from an atomic blast?

E-16: Why are the miners given drugs in *Outland*?

E-17: Ursula K. LeGuin's father was a famous anthropologist. Name him.

E-18: With what did Boris Karloff and Bela Lugosi experiment in *The Invisible Ray*?

E-19: In the 1952 film, how might one best describe *The Thing*?

E-20: What classic novel did Ray Bradbury reinterpret as *Leviathan 99*?

E-21: Name Edward G. Robinson's last film.

E-22: Name the robotic trio in *Silent Running*.

E-23: What does Ice Nine do?

E-24: If you lived on Arrakis, what would you probably wear?

E-25: What is Terraforming?

*(Answers appear on pages 170–71)*

# Bizarre Stuff

BS-1: Who possessed a Cosmic Vibrator, and just what did it do?

BS-2: According to Kurt Vonnegut, who plays shuffle-board in Heaven?

BS-3: What is Proteus IV, and what does it do to Julie Christie?

BS-4: From what is the title *Zardoz* derived?

BS-5: What is 42?

BS-6: Just who did the crew of the *Aries* encounter on Mars in the Philip José Farmer novel?

BS-7: What is Mr. Sardonicus' problem?

BS-8: If he ever makes the movie, what might John Landis call his dream project?

**What do Lectroids eat?**

BUCKAROO BANZAI PHOTO: COPYRIGHT © 1984 SHERWOOD PRODUCTIONS, INC.

BS-9: In what play does Willie the Space Freak appear?

BS-10: What movie has been described by its makers as both "Walt Disney on acid" and "Frank Capra meets *The Birds*"?

BS-11: Name the sequel (of sorts) to *The Rocky Horror Picture Show*.

BS-12: What was the most memorable special effect in David Cronenberg's *Scanners*?

BS-13: What was unusual about a certain human in the world of *Genesis II*?

BS-14: According to Larry Niven, what is rishathra?

BS-15: Who developed Smell-O-Vision?

BS-16: How many Topps bubble gum cards and stickers were released for *Mork and Mindy*?

BS-17: In Hugh Lofting's *Dr. Doolittle in the Moon*, how does the hero get to the Moon?

BS-18: In Jack Williamson's "Born of the Sun," what is the real purpose of the Earth?

BS-19: What was the secret of Bigfoot on *The Six Million Dollar Man*?

BS-20: In the John Carter series, how many arms does a green Martian have?

BS-21: Why were the protagonists of *Time Bandits* demoted by the Supreme Being?

BS-22: In one episode of *The Dick Van Dyke Show*, what did the flying saucer that visited Rob Petrie say?

BS-23: How did Woody Allen die in the film *Casino Royale*?

BS-24: What popular British comedian had a small character role in *Chitty Chitty Bang Bang*? And what author penned the original children's book?

BS-25: In what countries was *E.T.* banned for children?

*(Answers appear on pages 171–72)*

# Sword & Sorcery

**SO-1:** On what TV series would you find Prince Erik Grey-stone?

**SO-2:** Who created Conan?

**SO-3:** Who created *Dungeons and Dragons*?

**SO-4:** Of whom is the book *Dark Valley Destiny* a biography?

**SO-5:** In what film did *Hercules'* Lou Ferrigno and *Conan's* Arnold Schwarzenegger debut?

**SO-6:** What comics artist designed the characters in the Saturday morning animated series *Thundarr the Barbarian*?

**SO-7:** In what series of novels would one adventure on Counter-Earth?

**SO-8:** The characters F'lar and Lessa can be found in what series of books?

**SO-9:** Who chronicles the adventures of Fafhrd and the Grey Mouser?

**SO-10:** What's daringly different about the sword and sorcery character Jirel of Joiry?

**SO-11:** In what age was Conan a barbarian?

**SO-12:** What sort of complexion does Elric of Melnibone have?

**SO-13:** Name the town featured in the Thieves' World series.

**SO-14:** Who wields *Stormbringer*?

WIZARDS AND WARRIORS PHOTO: CBS

**Jeff Conaway (left above) and Walter Olkewicz shared satiric adventure in what short-lived sword & sorcery series?**

SO-15: "Sting" is the sword wielded by what famous character?

SO-16: What character from the King Kull stories appears in the Conan films?

SO-17: Name the writers who have written (or rewritten) novel (or short story) adventures of Conan after the creator's death.

SO-18: "The furball from hell" (created by Mark E. Rogers) is just a nickname for who?

SO-19: This writer has traveled to the World's End, enjoyed the Green Star's glow and sent Thongor the Barbarian into battle.

SO-20: The most successful satiric sword and sorcery series is published in Canada. Who is its creator? And what's remarkable about his variation on the Conan formula?

SO-21: The book shelves are full of sword and sorcery characters like Princess

Cija, Brak the Barbarian, Kane, Solomon Kane, Kothar, and Dorian Hawkmoon. And—you guessed it—which author created which character?

SO-22: What paperback phenomenon (and TV project) is the author of the Brak the Barbarian series best known for writing?

SO-23: What would you call a doctor with the Eye of Agamotto?

SO-24: According to Michael Moorcock, which of his characters are aspects of the Eternal Champion?

SO-25: Conan's greatest loves were Zenobia and Belit, but who was his greatest enemy?

*(Answers appear on pages 172–73)*

# Star Wars

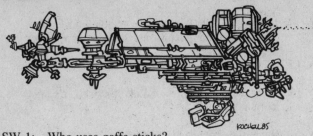

SW-1: Who uses gaffe sticks?

SW-2: On what planet do we first meet Luke Skywalker?

SW-3: What does TIE stand for in TIE fighter?

SW-4: For what purpose was C-3PO designed?

SW-5: On what date did *Star Wars* premiere?

SW-6: What actor appeared in both *Star Wars* and *Sinbad and the Eye of the Tiger*?

SW-7: What science-fiction writer co-scripted *The Big Sleep* (1946)?

SW-8: In what substance was Han Solo encased during his period of frozen suspended animation in *The Empire Strikes Back*?

SW-9: Who was the bounty hunter who brought Han Solo to Jabba the Hutt? And who portrayed him?

SW-10: What Peter Shaffer play did Mark Hamill appear in on Broadway? What role did Hamill portray?

SW-11: Name the Ewok who befriended Princess Leia.

SW-12: Name two teddy-bear-like creatures which predate the creation of the Ewoks.

SW-13: On what radio network did *The Empire Strikes Back* appear?

SW-14: In the first *Star Wars* Topps bubble gum card series, how many cards and stickers were there?

SW-15: Of what planet was Yoda a native?

SW-16: What were the names of Luke Skywalker's aunt and uncle?

SW-17: Name the writer and artist of the Marvel Comics adaptation of the original *Star Wars* movie.

SW-18: In a scene from *Star Wars* that wound up on the cutting room floor, Luke says goodbye to a friend who leaves Tatooine to join the alliance. Name this friend who *does* appear as one of the rebel pilots in the *Death Star* sequence.

SW-19: Cite the order in which the good guys appear on the screen in *Return of the Jedi.*

SW-20: In a time of emergency, what other character wielded Luke's light sabre? In what film? In what reel?

SW-21: What furry fact was revealed in the aired-only-once *Star Wars Christmas Special*?

SW-22: What does Leia ask Luke the first time they meet?

SW-23: What cast members of George Lucas' *American Graffiti* wanted to be Wookiees when they heard Lucas' early descriptions of the *Star Wars* saga?

SW-24: Is Grand Moff Tarkin true to his word?

SW-25: If *Star Wars V* is *The Empire Strikes Back* and *Stars Wars VI* is *Return of the Jedi*, what is *Star Wars IV*?

**SW-26:** Who flew the *Millennium Falcon* before Han Solo?

**SW-27:** What is Darth Vader's real name?

**SW-28:** You're walking along the sands of Tatooine with your lover. What makes the evening sky particularly romantic?

**SW-29:** In *Star Wars*, Leia tells Darth Vader that the rebel base is *where*?

**SW-30:** What is Darth Vader's royal title?

**SW-31:** This actor was Buckaroo Banzai's nemesis, but what was he to Luke Skywalker on *The Empire Strikes Back* radio show?

**Who portrayed these *characters* in the *Star Wars* radio series?**

EMPIRE STRIKES BACK PHOTO: COPYRIGHT © 1980 LUCASFILM LTD

SW-32: What are the odds of flying through an asteroid field?

SW-33: On Mos Eisley, where could one find the *Millennium Falcon*?

SW-34: Sylvester Stallone claims to have been offered what role for *Star Wars*?

SW-35: Who is the only background character to have survived all three *Star Wars*?

SW-36: Peter Cushing played Grand Moff Tarkin, but who was he originally approached to portray?

SW-37: What do the initials ILM stand for?

SW-38: According to the *Star Wars* radio show, what was the name of the star destroyer introduced in the fishing sequence?

SW-39: What actor portrayed both an Imperial officer and a Bond villain? What films? Which characters?

SW-40: What *Star Wars* saga actor had a minor role in *A Clockwork Orange*?

SW-41: During location lensing of *Return of the Jedi*, what was the production called to keep anxious fans away?

SW-42: What did Lawrence Kasdan and Harrison Ford have in mind for Han Solo in *Return of the Jedi*?

SW-43: What *Star Wars* merchandise appeared in *Poltergeist*?

SW-44: Who originally said, "I've got a bad feeling about this," in *Star Wars*? When? Who repeated it in the following episodes?

SW-45: George Lucas did not originally intend to make *Star Wars*. What was the SF series that he was unable to obtain the rights to?

SW-46: In order to escape the critics' assault on *Star Wars* and the traumas of the film's openings, George Lucas fled to Hawaii. Who did he meet there and what other popular movie series emerged from this rendezvous?

SW-47: What was Harrison Ford's first movie role?

SW-48: *Star Wars* composer John Williams also did music for what three SF-TV series?

SW-49: On *Leave it to Beaver*, which *Star Wars* star played the Beaver's best friend for a time?

SW-50: What inspiring message did President Reagan convey to Sally Ride during her voyage into space?

(Answers appear on pages 174–75)

# Irwin Allen Fun

IA-1: What was the name of the ship which was *Lost in Space*?

IA-2: Who played the tiny, fat villain in *Land of the Giants*?

IA-3: In what submarine would you take a *Voyage to the Bottom of the Sea*?

IA-4: What is Dr. Smith's first name?

IA-5: Walter Pidgeon and Richard Basehart. Both played what role? Don't forget the first name!

IA-6: Who was Dr. Smith working for when he first sabotaged the *Jupiter 2*?

IA-7: What was the name of the spacecraft in *Land of the Giants*?

IA-8: What model was the Robot in *Lost in Space*?

IA-9: Name the two-man explorer and the mini-sub added to the complement of the submarine in *Voyage to the Bottom of the Sea*.

IA-10: Who supplied the voice of the Robot in *Lost in Space*? Who operated the Robot?

IA-11: Who was captain of the *Voyage* submarine?

IA-12: *Lost in Space*'s Professor John Robinson rose to fame first playing what hero for Walt Disney? And in what color did he dress?

IA-13: Name the entire official crew of the *Jupiter 2*.

IA-14: What do the *Star Wars* saga, *E.T.*, *Dracula* and *Gilligan's Island* have in common with *Lost in Space*, *The Time Tunnel*, *Land of the Giants* and *The Towering Inferno*?

IA-15: Who was the recurring "special guest star" *Lost in Space*?

IA-16: In what years did *Land of the Giants* and *Lost in Space* take place?

IA-17: Where was the ship headed when it got lost in *Land of the Giants*?

IA-18: What do *Voyage to the Bottom of the Sea* and the James Bond movie *Live and Let Die* have in common?

IA-19: Where do the heroes of *The Time Tunnel* appear in the first and last episodes?

IA-20: "The Price of Doom" was the title of the episode written by Harlan Ellison for what Allen series?

IA-21: It was a very good thing, a very good thing that Bill Mumy made an appearance in this SF fantasy series. What was the series?

IA-22: Which cast member from *Lost in Space* had a daughter who would go on to star in another SF series? Name the offspring and the show.

IA-23: "Pay the Piper" from *Land of the Giants* guest starred which *Lost in Space* actor?

IA-24: The *Jupiter 2*'s land vehicle was called the. . .

IA-25: On *Voyage to the Bottom of the Sea*, what role did the star of *The Fly* have?

*(Answers appear on pages 175-76)*

# Apes and Primates

AP-1: Who scripted the film *Planet of the Apes*?

AP-2: What destroyed the Earth in *Beneath the Planet of the Apes*?

AP-3: Who wrote the book *Planet of the Apes*? What was its original title?

AP-4: He designed the Oscar-winning makeup for the apes in *Planet of the Apes*. Name him.

AP-5: Who is Moonwatcher?

AP-6: A killer ape figured prominently in what famed Edgar Allan Poe detective story?

AP-7: In what film does the star of *Eyewitness* regress to primal man state and spend the night in the zoo?

AP-8: The Flash fought a hairy genius from a race of super-intelligent beings in Africa. Name this comic book villain.

AP-9: What enraged the captive *King Kong* (1933) during his sell-out performance in New York?

AP-10: According to publicity, 30 bears sacrificed their furs for whom?

AP-11: According to *The Creation of Dino De Laurentiis'
King Kong*, the role of Dwan was originally conceived for what actress?

AP-12: What three roles did Roddy McDowall play in the
*Planet of the Apes* film/TV series?

AP-13: On the *Planet of the Apes*, gorillas mainly comprised what class?

AP-14: Who, respectively, were the bureaucrats and scientists of the *Planet of the Apes*?

AP-15: Scientist Michael Gough grew a monkey into a giant
ape which terrorized London. And what did they
call this ape?

AP-16: In the films and TV series, the *Planet of the Apes*
was Earth. However, in the book, what was the
planet called?

AP-17: Tarzan was raised by apes. Who raised Lucan in
that TV series?

AP-18: The classic movie score for *King Kong* was composed by . . . ?

AP-19: What is the name of the apelike race used by the
Daleks in "Day of the Daleks" on *Doctor Who*?

AP-20: Who played Urko in TV's *Planet of the Apes*?

AP-21: Where was *Mighty Joe Young* exhibited?

AP-22: The killer ape in *Schlock* left what telltale clue at
the scenes of his crimes?

AP-23: Unhappy with his treatment on Dino De Laurentiis'
*King Kong*, makeup artist Rick Baker may have had
a last laugh in *Kentucky Fried Movie*. How?

AP-24: In what comedy did Rick Baker portray a love-sick gorilla?

AP-25: In 1963's *King Kong vs. Godzilla*, the two monsters battled. And who triumphed?

*(Answers appear on pages 176–77)*

**Name this actor and actress from the *Planet of the Apes*.**

PLANET OF THE APES PHOTOS: 20TH CENTURY FOX

# SF Women

W-1: Who was *The Bionic Woman*?

W-2: Julie Newmar, Lee Meriwether and Eartha Kitt. What feline role did they share?

W-3: Who plays *Stella Star*?

W-4: What is the name given the mermaid in *Splash*?

W-5: What could Drew Barrymore do in *Firestarter*?

W-6: Why is *The Bionic Woman* bionic?

W-7: In a film, she reveals that her father died in a chimney. Who is she?

W-8: In what movie would you find Fatima Blush?

W-9: Who plays Supergirl?

W-10: What actress held the love interest of *Swamp Thing*?

W-11: In what film does Natassja Kinski develop a taste for live rabbit?

W-12: Who is Mentor's daughter?

W-13: In *The Girl with Something Extra*, what was that "something extra"?

W-14: If Wonder Woman wanted to go home for the holidays, where would she go?

W-15: What actress did Lou Ferrigno battle in *Hercules*?

W-16: Who wrote *The Left Hand of Darkness*

and *The Lathe of Heaven*?

Dorothy in *Return to Oz*?

W-17: To whom does Princess Aura send a card on Father's Day?

W-18: Who is She-Who-Must-Be-Obeyed?

W-19: Who did MGM first want to play Dorothy in *The Wizard of Oz*?

W-20: Who plays *Red Sonja*?

W-21: This fantasy artist is best known by her first name, Rowena. What's her last name?

W-22: And who is Disney's

W-23: She was *Willard*'s mother, *The Bride of Frankenstein* and (in real life) Charles Laughton's wife. And her name?

W-24: Raquel Welch got small in one film and went prehistoric in another. What were those movies?

W-25: She palled around with Robby the Robot (in *Forbidden Planet*) and came alive as a mannequin (in *The Twilight Zone*). Name the actress.

*(Answers appear on pages 177–78)*

**"It knows what scares you." What is it? And who is this SF woman?**

POLTERGEIST PHOTO: COPYRIGHT © 1982 MGM/UA AND SLM ENTERTAINMENT

# The Doctor

DOCTOR WHO PHOTO: COPYRIGHT © BBC

Tom Baker is the Doctor. But who's his companion?

D-1: What two actors voiced K-9?

D-2: What is the meaning of TARDIS?

D-3: Who created *Doctor Who*?

D-4: Colin Baker, the sixth Doctor Who, appeared in what previous episode of the series?

D-5: What does UNIT stand for?

D-6: What is Brigadier Lethbridge-Stewart's first name?

D-7: What planet did the Doctor steal the Blue Crystal from?

D-8: Who was the Doctor's first assistant at UNIT?

D-9: Why did Jo Grant leave the Doctor?

D-10: With the exception of John Nathan-Turner, who produced the program for the longest time?

D-11: Which of the Doctor's companions was also a doctor? And who portrayed him?

D-12: What race gradually exchanged their vital organs for metal and plastic replacements?

D-13: What writer created the Daleks?

D-14: Who designed the Daleks?

D-15: Who were the Doctor's original three companions?

D-16: On what planet did the First Doctor discover Vicki?

D-17: What one-story companion was assigned to kill the Doctor but ended up helping him?

D-18: Who assigned her to kill the Doctor?

D-19: What other companion was sent to kill the Doctor, and who ordered him to do this?

D-20: What was the name of the locust-like creatures in "The Ark in Space?"

D-21: What was the nickname of "The Mutants?"

D-22: What instrument did the Second Doctor play?

D-23: What are the Cybermen's "pets" called?

D-24: What race clones itself?

D-25: What was the name of the alien the

Doctor and Sarah encountered in the middle ages? Name the episode.

D-26: What is the name of the Martian race?

D-27: What substance is mined on Peladon?

D-28: What was the name of "The Monster of Peladon?"

D-29: What was the Fourth Doctor's favorite sweet?

D-30: What metal is fatal to Cybermen?

D-31: Name the planet of gold.

D-32: What was the name of "The Web Planet?"

D-33: Name the two dominant life forms on "The Web Planet" and the organism which controls them.

D-34: What was Sarah Jane Smith's occupation?

D-35: Name the Dalek play written by Terry

Nation and David Whitaker.

D-36: Name the four actors who have played the Master.

D-37: Who produced *Doctor Who* for the first three TV seasons?

D-38: What aliens did the Doctor find at Loch Ness?

D-39: What was the name of the alien plant creature in "Seeds of Death?"

D-40: Who played Adric?

D-41: Why was Adric given his badge?

D-42: In what episode was Adric killed?

D-43: What was unique about this episode's credit sequence?

D-44: Who wrote the title theme of the program?

D-45: What was the name of the first story? What was the alternate title of episodes two through four?

D-46: In which story did the Cybermen first appear? What significant event took place in the final episode?

D-47: What two planets were home to the Cybermen?

D-48: What was the name of King Peladon's daughter?

D-49: What episode was never completed or aired?

D-50: What was the name of the ill-fated feature film co-scripted by Tom Baker and Ian Marter?

*(Answers appear on pages 178–79)*

**Which doctor is represented by a dummy?**

DOCTOR WHO PHOTO: COPYRIGHT © BBC

# Funny Stuff

FS-1: Who does Emperor Wang battle?

FS-2: In what film might you experience the joys of the Orgasmatron?

FS-3: Who created *The Hitchhiker's Guide to the Galaxy*?

FS-4: Identify the crew of the spaceship *Swinetrek*.

FS-5: Name the ship housing the Improbability Drive.

FS-6: Who created *Quark*?

FS-7: What fictitious SF film was previewed at the end of Mel Brooks' *History of the World (Part One)*?

FS-8: What famous SF director makes a brief appearance near the climax of *The Blues Brothers*?

FS-9: What happens when *Bambi Meets Godzilla*?

**3 STOOGES IN ORBIT (1962)**

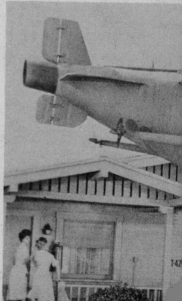

FS-10: What is the chosen instrument of Earth's annihilation opposed by *Ghostbusters*?

FS-11: Who portrayed TV's *Captain Nice*?

FS-12: Who plays the country bumpkin Jordy Verrill in the film *Creepshow*?

FS-13: In what substance was Woody Allen encased during his period of frozen suspended animation in *Sleeper*?

FS-14: Name Groucho Marx's TV announcer. The secret word is the SF film classic in which he appeared.

FS-15: What SF comedy was the last full-length feature film appearance of Andy Kaufman?

FS-16: What film has been

There are several captains of this vessel. Who are they?

described as "the black *E.T.*?"

FS-17: In what film would you find the characters Buck Murdock, Elaine Dickinson and Ted Striker?

FS-18: In *Splash*, what magazine prints a letter written by John Candy's character?

FS-19: What book's alternate title was *Lonesome No More!*?

FS-20: In what film did the Duchy of Grand Fenwick send an expedition into outer space?

FS-21: What was Marvin the Android's problem?

FS-22: Who was *The Reluctant Astronaut*?

FS-23: In *Superman III*, Richard Pryor takes the final ingredient for synthetic Kryptonite from what?

FS-24: Who directed *Time Bandits*?

FS-25: What runs the country in the world of Woody Allen's *Sleeper*?

*(Answers appear on page 180)*

# Battlestar Galactica

BG-1: Name Boxy's pet robot daggit.

BG-2: Define "Felkercarb."

BG-3: What was the *Galactica* jargon equivalent of a minute?

BG-4: Who was Adama's second-in-command in the first series?

BG-5: How many episodes were there in the first season?

BG-6: On what night of the week and what network was *Battlestar Galactica* broadcast?

BG-7: What were the ranks of Apollo and Starbuck, respectively?

BG-8: Who created *Battlestar Galactica*?

BG-9: What was the name of Captain Apollo's wife, and what was her profession?

BG-10: When we met her, what was Cassiopea's profession?

BG-11: Name the warrior race who went on occasional blood hunts.

BG-12: Who portrayed the legendary military leader Commander Cain?

BG-13: What character did *St. Elsewhere*'s Ed Begley, Jr. play on *Galactica*?

BG-14: What squadron did Commander Cain's daughter belong to? What was her name?

BG-15: Producer Don Bellisario went on to create what *three* subsequent TV adventure series?

BG-16: Name the *Galactica*'s attack craft.

BG-17: How many Battlestars were there in the original fleet?

**Whose voice was behind the Imperious Leader?**

GALACTICA PHOTO: COPYRIGHT © 1979 UNIVERSAL CITY STUDIOS

BG-18: Early in *Battlestar Galactica*'s storyline, what pivotal character died?

BG-19: What villain in *Battlestar Galactica* was originally killed in the theatrical feature version released in Canada, but was restored to life (through the magic of editing) for the U.S. series?

BG-20: Who played Starbuck's father in one episode of *Battlestar Galactica*?

BG-21: How many Cylons sit in a fighter?

BG-22: The robot Cylons were created by a race of what kind of animal?

BG-23: How many of the original fleet of Battlestars survived the Cylon ambush?

BG-24: After *Battlestar Galactica*'s cancellation, tourists could still encounter Cylons at what California attraction?

BG-25: Name the actor who was both the heavy on *Battlestar Galactica* and on *Star Trek* as a Klingon.

*(Answers appear on pages 180–81)*

**How many Oscars did E.T. take home?**

# Oscars & Honors

**O-1:** Who won special Oscars for *Fantasia*?

**O-2:** For whom are the Hugo awards named (and it's *not* Victor Hugo)?

**O-3:** *The Duellists* was what SF filmmaker's award-winning first film?

**O-4:** Who was the first motion picture artist to be honored with a solo gallery exhibition at New York's

Museum of Modern Art?

O-5: What museum will you find in Wapokoneta, Ohio?

O-6: The John W. Campbell Award is awarded to whom?

O-7: Who is the only *director* to win three Hugos for Best Dramatic Presentation? Name the films.

O-8: What TV series won the Hugo for Best Dramatic Presentation *three* years in a row?

O-9: Name the major SF literature awards.

O-10: Name the only author to win joint Hugo and Nebula awards for best SF novel of the year on *two* separate occasions.

O-11: Joe Haldeman won a Nebula and a Hugo for his novel about a future military struggle. Name the book.

O-12: Who was the first person awarded a regular Oscar for Best Makeup Effects?

O-13: For what role was Edmund Gwenn gifted with an Oscar?

O-14: Ruth Gordon won an Oscar for her supporting role in what film?

O-15: In 1969, Neil Armstrong, Edwin Aldrin and Michael Collins were awarded a Special Hugo for what?

O-16: Did you hear James Bond won an Oscar in 1964? What for?

O-17: Believe it or not, this 1976 critical and box-office failure actually won the Oscar for special visual effects. Name it.

O-18: True or false: Both *Star Wars* and *Close Encounters of the Third Kind* were nominated for the 1977 Best Picture Oscar.

O-19: So, how many Oscars did *Star Wars* win anyway?

O-20: The Hugo awards

were initiated in 1953, but what is unusual about the 1954 list of recipients?

O-21: True or false: *Star Trek—The Motion Picture* won *no* Academy Awards.

O-22: Who composed the award-winning original score for *The Omen*?

O-23: How many people shared the honors for *Superman's* award-winning visual effects?

O-24: What do *Jaws, Star Trek, Raiders of the Lost Ark* and *Mary Poppins* have in common?

O-25: The TV producers bowdlerized the script, but that's OK because this author's *original* pilot teleplay, "Phoenix Without Ashes," won a Nebula award anyway. Name the author and the TV series.

*(Answers appear on pages 181–82)*

# The Written Word

KOCHELL

**WW-1:** Who penned *The Stepford Wives* and *The Boys from Brazil*?

**WW-2:** What science had the Chinese perfected in Kurt Vonnegut's *Slapstick*?

**WW-3:** Who is Eric Blair?

**WW-4:** Under what pen name did *Under the Moons of Mars* first appear?

**WW-5:** In Heinlein's Future Histories, who is the world's oldest man?

**WW-6:** If Harlan Ellison were to write *Star Trek* today, he says, the first thing he would do is . . . ?

**WW-7:** Who wrote *Venus on the Half-Shell*?

**WW-8:** *Destination Moon* involved what science-fiction writer with Hollywood?

**WW-9:** Who received screenplay credit for *Altered States*?

**WW-10:** Under what pseudonym is the late American writer Charles Nutt better known?

**WW-11:** Who created Dominic Flandry?

**WW-12:** What American writer wrote a book whose title became the imprint for a line of mass market paperbacks? Also, name the book.

**WW-13:** He edited both *Analog* and *Omni*. Name this blue-pencil wielding SF author.

**WW-14:** Who created Jimgrim and King of the Khyber Rifles?

**WW-15:** Why was Arkham House founded?

**WW-16:** Name the creator of The Skylark of Space and The Lensman.

**WW-17:** Who wrote the *Majipoor Chronicles*?

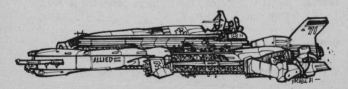

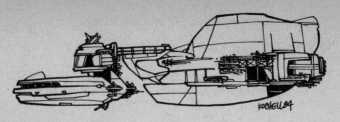

WW-18: *The Iron Dream* by Norman Spinrad was banned in what country?

WW-19: What is the only non-fiction book written by Stephen King?

WW-20: Upon what book was the TV series *Tom Corbett, Space Cadet* based?

WW-21: What Philip Wylie novel lent inspiration to the creation of Superman?

WW-22: What American president announced he enjoyed reading an adventure series by a British writer, thereby prompting a sales surge in the series? Name the series, as well.

WW-23: *Shatterday* was a collection of short stories by what author?

WW-24: In *The Lion, the Witch and the Wardrobe*, how does one get to Narnia?

WW-25: Name any five of the 15 winners of the Nobel Prize in Literature who have written SF or fantasy.

WW-26: "If Lincoln Had Not Lost at Gettysburg" was an alternate history written by what world leader?

WW-27: Name Frank Herbert's first novel.

WW-28: *A Spell for Chameleon, Centaur Isle, Night Mare* and other Piers Anthony books are set where?

WW-29: What was Walter Miller's first novel?

WW-30: Who chronicled the life of "The People?"

WW-31: A close encounter between humans and an intelligent cloud of interstellar gas can be found in what classic SF novel?

WW-32: What SF writer founded a real-life religion?

WW-33: Charles Dodgson is the real name of what author?

WW-34: Of his own work, what is Isaac Asimov's favorite novel (thus far)?

WW-35: *Last and First Man, Star Maker* and *Odd John* are the work of English philosopher and SF writer . . . ?

WW-36: What were the Futurians?

WW-37: Who wrote the screenplay for *The Invisible Man* (1938)?

WW-38: Name the films adapted from the *novels* of Ray Bradbury.

WW-39: What is the real title of *Gulliver's Travels*?

WW-40: He wrote *Binary*. He directed *The Great Train Robbery* (1979). He computer-designed *Amazon*. Who is he?

KING KONG PHOTO: COPYRIGHT © 1933 RKO PICTURES

**What famous mystery writer was associated with the novelization of *King Kong*?**

WW-41: On what short story are both film versions of *The Thing* based?

WW-42: What is the subtitle of Mary Shelley's *Frankenstein*?

WW-43: L. Frank Baum. What does the "L" stand for?

WW-44: Who is Richard Bachman?

WW-45: John Varley's Gaea Trilogy is comprised of which books?

WW-46: In Thomas M. Disch's short story "102 H-Bombs," what 20th century artifact is actually a time machine?

WW-47: Grim Friddle is conceived in a bar called "The Mickey Mouse Club" in what John Calvin Batchelor novel?

WW-48: In Mervyn Peake's *Gormenghast* trilogy, what is "gormenghast?"

WW-49: What did the Ticktockman say?

WW-50: Who penned the original novels *The Night Stalker* and *The Night Strangler*?

*(Answers appear on pages 182–84)*

# Twilight Zone

TZ-1: On what night of the week during its first season was *The Twilight Zone* aired?

TZ-2: What is the title of the episode in which "The Sundance Kid" played Death?

TZ-3: Who broke his glasses on the library steps after massive nuclear destruction?

TZ-4: Burt Lancaster's acrobatic ex-partner terrorized a discharged mental patient in this classic episode.

TZ-5: Who was Helen Foley?

TZ-6: What is Rod Serling's home town?

TZ-7: What things did Flight 33 see that indicated they were off course?

TZ-8: In what year, and on what network did *The Twilight Zone* debut?

TZ-9: *Family Affair*'s Mr. French played Mr. Pip in which episode?

TZ-10: Ed Norton was Santa Claus in this episode.

TZ-11: What decorated the top of the all-knowing fortune telling machine in "Nick of Time"?

TZ-12: Who was the last of "The Passersby"?

TZ-13: One *Twilight Zone* writer went on to create what famous CBS homespun drama?

In this episode, Jack Weston (right) urges on a famous writer (actor John Williams). Who did Williams portray?

TWILIGHT ZONE PHOTO: CBS

TZ-14: How many tiny men terrorized Agnes Moorehead in "The Invaders"?

TZ-15: To save his business, what does Lee Marvin do in "Steel"?

TZ-16: How many arms does a *real* Martian have, and how many eyes, a Venusian?

TZ-17: How does Grandma Bayles contact Little Billy from beyond the grave?

TZ-18: To whom does used car salesman Jack Carson sell a haunted Ford Model A?

TZ-19: Why does Ed Wynn make the big pitch, "One for the Angels"?

TZ-20: In what department of a Kanamit book store might you find the volume *To Serve Man*?

TZ-21: What was the gift of "The Purple Testament"?

TZ-22: What was the only Ray Bradbury short story to appear as a *Twilight Zone* episode?

TZ-23: What was Anne Francis in "The After Hours"?

TZ-24: What was "The Occurrence at Owl Creek Bridge"?

TZ-25: Name the three original *Twilight Zone* episodes reinterpreted in *Twilight Zone the Movie*?

*(Answers appear on pages 184–85)*

# Classics

C-1: What ship did Robur, *Master of the World*, command?

C-2: What is the planet Altair-4 also known as?

C-3: How many spirits visited Scrooge on Christmas Eve?

C-4: Who did Montressor brick up in the wall in Poe's "The Cask of Amontillado?"

C-5: Name the Brothers Grimm.

C-6: Who was chased out of Sleepy Hollow by the Headless Horseman?

C-7: "Farewell to the Master," by Harry Bates, is the basis for what film? In the story, *who* was the master?

C-8: What does Dorian Gray keep in his attic?

C-9: How long was Jules Verne's fictional trip in a balloon?

C-10: As an RAF pilot, he created the concept of "gremlins." He later married an actress who starred in an SF classic. Name him, her, and the movie.

C-11: Who was Quasimodo?

C-12: *The Day the Earth Stood Still* and *Lost Horizon* (1937). What actor appeared in both?

C-13: What silent filmmaker can be considered the *first* SF director?

C-14: How was Captain Nemo's submarine powered in the Disney film version of *20,000 Leagues Under the Sea*?

C-15: Name the *first* SF film.

**What classic novel is Khan fond of quoting?**

STAR TREK II PHOTO: COPYRIGHT © 1982 PARAMOUNT PICTURES, INC.

C-16: What was the first screen adaptation of the Bram Stoker novel *Dracula*?

C-17: What was Richard Matheson's first produced screenplay?

C-18: From what nation did Jules Verne hail?

C-19: Shakespeare's *The Tempest* was refashioned into what SF classic?

C-20: Who starred in Don Siegel's *Invasion of the Body Snatchers* (1956)?

C-21: Who played the doubting little girl in the original *Miracle on 34th Street*?

C-22: What famous director performed in *Close Encounters of the Third Kind*?

C-23: In *Theatre of Blood*, the murders were patterned after whose plays?

C-24: How do Jules Verne's castaways find themselves marooned on *The Mysterious Island*?

C-25: Who directed *Silent Running*?

*(Answers appear on pages 185–86)*

# Songs & Sounds

**SO-1:** To whom does *The Next Voice You Hear* belong?

**SO-2:** What happens when you speak the name of a Sandgorgon?

**SO-3:** Who composed the scores for *The Day the Earth Stood Still*, *Journey to the Center of the Earth*, *The Seventh Voyage of Sinbad* and *Psycho*?

**SO-4:** What's unusual about the actor who played Rand Peltzer, the father in *Gremlins*?

**SO-5:** Who supplied the grunts and growls for TV's live-action *Incredible Hulk*?

**SO-6:** Who supplied the vocalizations of Gizmo in *Gremlins*?

**SO-7:** Which pop music star played a sleazy pop psychologist in *Videodrome*?

**SO-8:** Who composed the music scores of *The Fury, Dracula (1979), 1941* and *Superman*?

**SO-9:** What composer scored *Coma, Logan's Run, ALIEN* and *The Swarm*?

**SO-10:** Who was Robert Heinlein's Blind Singer of the Spaceways in *The Green Hills of Earth* (1947)?

**SO-11:** On what TV series would you hear the "Funeral March of a Marionette?"

**SO-12:** Alexander Courage composed the theme for what SF TV series?

SO-13: How did Earth defeat the aliens in *Earth Versus the Flying Saucers*?

SO-14: Name the SF hit o

the rock group Zager and Evans.

SO-15: Who "Set the Controls for the Heart of the Sun?''

**Who wrote Willie Scott's opening number? And what's the song?**

INDIANA JONES PHOTO: COPYRIGHT © 1984 PARAMOUNT PICTURES, INC

SO-16: Who sang "Mars ain't the kind of place you raise your kids?"

SO-17: What Rick Springfield video has an SF theme?

SO-18: Walter Carlos arranged the music for *A Clockwork Orange*. Wendy Carlos composed the music for *TRON*. Are they related?

SO-19: The film *Doc Savage—The Man of Bronze* featured the music of what composer?

SO-20: What popular song was used, perhaps a bit incongruously, in *A Clockwork Orange*?

SO-21: In a nonsense song, what do ladies do in a bar on Mars?

SO-22: What does SHADO stand for?

SO-23: How do you do the Time Warp (as illustrated in *The Rocky Horror Picture Show*)?

SO-24: Where did the "sweet transvestite" come from in *Rocky Horror*?

SO-25: And what (if anything) can be said to be the message of *The Rocky Horror Picture Show*?

*(Answers appear on pages 186–87)*

# Animations of Life

AL-1: Who were Space Ghost's three friends?

AL-2: Who was the pilot of *Fireball XL5*?

AL-3: Why was Astro Boy created?

AL-4: If you were Mike Mercury, what would you be driving?

AL-5: Where did Underdog get his power?

AL-6: What film featured Terry Thomas, Buddy Hackett, a dragon and elves (animated, in part, by Jim Danforth)?

AL-7: Who was the voice of Space Ghost?

AL-8: The wooden marionette faces a space whale in what 1964 animated film?

AL-9: Ray Harryhausen animated the Venusian in *20 Million Miles to Earth*. Name it.

AL-10: Director Richard Fleischer is related to what legendary film figures?

AL-11: What made the unusual journey (where no project had gone before) from TV series to cartoon series to film?

AL-12: In which Jim Henson movie did *no* Muppets appear?

AL-13: What game show host voiced The Man of Steel in cartoons and radio?

AL-14: Walter E. Disney. What does the "E." stand for?

AL-15: Name Walt Disney's Seven Dwarfs.

AL-16: WASP stands for . . . ?

AL-17: Who was the little green pest from outer space who made life generally miserable for Fred Flintstone and Barney Rubble? And who supplied his voice?

AL-18: Where did George Jetson work?

AL-19: What did the evil wizard in *Wizards* use to incite his followers?

AL-20: How did good triumph over evil in *Wizards*?

AL-21: Who was "the science-fiction pixie from a strange atomic race"?

AL-22: What SF cartoon had the distinction of superimposing human lips on animated faces?

AL-23: Who rides Battle Cat and fights Skeletor?

AL-24: What was Mad Madam Mim's favorite color?

GREMLINS PHOTO: COPYRIGHT © 1984 WARNER BROS. INC.

**What animation legend is that sitting next to Zach Galligan in _Gremlins_?**

AL-25: In _The Secret of NIMH_, what did NIMH stand for?

AL-26: Hadjii was whose best friend?

AL-27: Name the two video games that animator Don Bluth and his colleagues devised.

AL-28: Who was Mr. Spacely's chief competitor on _The Jetsons_?

AL-29: Name the segments of the _Heavy Metal_ film.

AL-30: Who was Gumby's horse? What color was he?

AL-31: What was the name of the food preparation device on _The Jetsons_?

AL-32: What time-space continuum did Hoppity Hooper and his friends enter?

AL-33: Who created Frankenstein Jr.?

AL-34: Who was Dr. Benton Quest's arch-foe?

AL-35: How did Marine Boy breathe underwater?

AL-36: She-Ra has a famous twin-brother, who is he?

AL-37: What army task force is named after a *real* American hero?

AL-38: Which famous Japanese robot preceeded Voltron, Transformers and the Go-Bots?

AL-39: The Tracy family formed International Rescue on which British TV series?

AL-40: Col. White, Lt. Green and Harmony Angel belong to which Gerry Anderson show?

**Duck Dodgers goes to Planet X to find a new supply of Aludium Q-36. What is it?**

DUCK DODGERS PHOTO: COPYRIGHT © 1953 WARNER BROS.

AL-41: Name the starship in the imported Japanese animated series *Star Blazers*?

AL-42: Who was *8th Man*?

AL-43: Bugs Bunny outwitted hunter Elmer Fudd and nemesis Daffy Duck—much to the misplacement of Daffy's beak—in a trilogy of Chuck Jones cartoons. Name them.

AL-44: What northwestern town do Rocky and Bullwinkle call home?

AL-45: And where did Bullwinkle go to college?

AL-46: What does *Underdog* have in common with *The Rocky Horror Picture Show*!?

AL-47: Which "Superfriend" is voiced by *American Top 40*'s Casey Kasem?

AL-48: Who commands the good ship *Arcadia*?

AL-49: A voice sings, "Here I come to save the day!" What does it mean?

AL-50: Who voiced Corey, the master of *Jeannie*, in the Hanna-Barbera cartoon?

*(Answers appear on pages 187–89)*

# SF TV

SF-1: *Captain Video and His Video Rangers* appeared on what television network?

SF-2: What was Roj Blake's vocation?

SF-3: Name two invisible men who had their own television series.

SF-4: Who played Arthur Dent in the TV version of *The Hitchhiker's Guide to the Galaxy*?

SF-5: What actor (who appeared in *Forbidden Planet*) played the same role in two television series both airing at the *same* time—and for a while, broadcast on different networks?

SF-6: What television series did Cordwainer Bird create?

**Believe it or not, this man does not have four hands. What TV movie earned his first critical accolades?**

SPIELBERG PHOTO: COPYRIGHT © 1975 UNIVERSAL PICTURES

SF-7: What is the *Liberator*?

SF-8: Where would you find Moonbase Alpha?

SF-9: Who is Rem?

SF-10: What happens when Dr. David Bruce Banner gets mad?

SF-11: Wernher Von Braun was the technical consultant on "Man in Space," "Man in the Moon," and "Mars and Beyond," all segments of what popular TV show?

SF-12: In what TV series does the submarine-research vessel *Cetacean* appear?

SF-13: Where might one find an Eagle spacecraft?

SF-14: What were the occupations, respectively, of Ralph Hinkley and Bill Maxwell of *The Greatest American Hero*?

SF-15: What was the planned title of *Space: 1999*?

SF-16: Who is *The Seven Million Dollar Man*?

SF-17: What was Paul Newman's first appearance on television?

SF-18: In what TV series might you find the characters Buzz Corey and Cadet Happy?

SF-19: Name the two actors who played Darren Stevens in *Bewitched*.

SF-20: Who were *Sapphire and Steel*?

SF-21: Dr. Fred Walters joined *The Fantastic Journey* by getting lost in what area?

SF-22: The Sterlings visited the *Otherworld* by getting lost where?

SF-23: On how many networks did *Tom Corbett, Space Cadet* appear?

SF-24: For what organization did Buzz Corey work?

SF-25: Who was Mr. Wizard?

*(Answers appear on pages 189–90)*

# Wondrous Worlds

WO-1: In *First Men in the Moon*, what are the race of moon men called?

WO-2: Where would you find the *Nautilus*?

WO-3: By the way, what was the name of Jules Verne's yacht?

WO-4: In what movie would you find Centauri and Grig?

WO-5: In *Foundation's Edge*, who wins the conflict among the First Foundation, the Second Foundation and Gaia?

WO-6: In a series of Robert Heinlein stories, what replaced highways and cars in America during the 1950s and 1960s?

WO-7: What film was referred to as the "Froud Project?"

WO-8: *Night Skies* and *A Boy's Life* were early titles for a project which later metamorphosized into what?

**What is the relationship between the Skeksis and the Mystics?**

DARK CRYSTAL PHOTO: COPYRIGHT © 1981 ITC ENTERTAINMENT

WO-9: Who are the three main characters of the video game *Space Ace*?

WO-10: Name the three books in C.S. Lewis' space series.

WO-11: Of what race is Jen, the only hope for the world of *The Dark Crystal*?

WO-12: Name the Brothers Hildebrandt.

WO-13: What are the names of the four ghosts in *Pac-Man*?

WO-14: Neal Adams designed visual material for what multi-part SF stage show?

WO-15: What is *The Land that Time Forgot*? Where is it?

WO-16: In the C.S. Lewis space series, what are the dancers before the threshold of the Great Worlds?

WO-17: Who resided in the *House of Frankenstein*?

WO-18: Where did Abbott and Costello go in 1953?

WO-19: What does J.R.R. stand for in the name J.R.R. Tolkien?

WO-20: Name the brass giant in *Jason and Argonauts*.

WO-21: *The Ship of Ishtar, The Metal Monster, Seven Footprints to Satan* and *The Dweller in the Mirage* were written by . . . ?

WO-22: In the book version of *The Wizard of Oz*, what color were Dorothy's slippers?

WO-23: In Ann McCaffrey's Dragonrider series, Pern is the third planet of what star?

WO-24: In what film do Landstriders and Pod People appear?

WO-25: A relaxing vacation in Delos would place you in what movie/TV series environment?

*(Answers appear on page 190)*

# Giant or Otherwise Unusual Animals

G-1: What was *Harvey*?

G-2: How many tentacles did the giant squid in Disney's *20,000 Leagues Under the Sea* have?

G-3: What small flightless birds did Dick Van Dyke dance with in *Mary Poppins*?

G-4: Who wrote *The Lost World*?

G-5: What were *Them*?

G-6: What was the incredible menace during the *Night of the Lepus*?

G-7: What three things don't you want to do to a Mogwai?

G-8: James (*Shogun*) Clavell scripted two genre films. Name them.

G-9: Who is Chris Walas?

G-10: How many tentacles did the mutant octopus of *It Came from Beneath the Sea* have?

G-11: What species ruled George Orwell's *Animal Farm*?

G-12: In what film did William Shatner co-star with some 5,000 live tarantulas?

G-13: What are "cute, clever, mischievous, intelligent, dangerous"?

G-14: Who was *Charly*'s best friend? And what was he?

G-15: What was the species name of the lovable, cuddly little animals seen in *Battlestar Galactica*?

G-16: He built Bruce the shark in *Jaws* and the squid in *20,000 Leagues Under the Sea*.

G-17: Name Dr. Doolittle's two-headed llama and his pet parrot.

G-18: What was the name of *The Cat from Outer Space*?

G-19: Where do Dragonriders ride?

G-20: What was the giant, jet-propelled, fire-breathing space turtle which terrorized Japan?

G-21: *The Beginning of the End* for Chicago came when a swarm of giant whats showed up?

G-22: If it was 1959 and you heard a tiny insect scream, "Help me! Help me," what would you do?

G-23: What is E.G. Marshall's greatest fear in *Creepshow*?

G-24: Name Godzilla's son.

G-25: What is the fatal weakness of those tomatoes in *Attack of the Killer Tomatoes*?

*(Answers appear on page 191)*

# See You in the Funny Papers

FP-1: Name the three actors who have portrayed Superman on the movie screen.

FP-2: Who accompanied Dr. G. Oscar Boom on his trip to the moon in 1957?

FP-3: Where would you find the Clown Prince of Crime?

FP-4: What are the only two things which will harm Superman?

FP-5: What was Green Lantern's oath?

FP-6: Name the three Phantom Zone villains who threatened the Earth in *Superman II*.

FP-7: Who created Donald Duck's Uncle Scrooge?

FP-8: Who was Wonder Woman's mom?

FP-9: What happens to Superman under a red sun?

FP-10: Is Supergirl related to Superman? If so, how?

FP-11: Who is the law in Mega-City One?

ANNIE PHOTO: COPYRIGHT © 1982 COLUMBIA PICTURES

The movie Annie was played by Aileen Quinn. Who was the first *Broadway* stage Annie?

FP-12: Who created the comic strip *Star Hawks*?

FP-13: How did Adam Strange get back and forth from Earth to Rann?

FP-14: In *Supergirl*, how does Superman (Christopher Reeve) cameo?

FP-15: Who was the bride of TV's *Incredible Hulk*?

FP:-16: Who wrote and drew the comic strip version of Edgar Rice Burroughs' *John Carter of Mars*?

FP-17: Jack Kirby pencilled an adaptation of which 1979 SF film?

FP-18: Who created Superman?

FP-19: What two things did aliens often say in EC science-fiction comics?

FP-20: What is Superman's real name?

FP-21: In the movie *Popeye*, in what seaport town does the action occur?

FP-22: In what did Brick Bradford travel to the past, present, and future?

FP-23: Who was Britain's "Pilot of the Future?"

FP-24: What is Galactus' favorite food?

FP-25: Who was the original herald serving Galactus?

FP-26: EC comics adapted the SF tales of what noted writer?

FP-27: Who was TV's *original* Wonder Woman?

FP-28: On what networks did *Wonder Woman* appear?

He's a legend. And he portrayed a legendary character. Who is he—and which comics superhero did he play?

PHOTO: JOHNNY LOWE

MICKEY'S CHRISTMAS CAROL. ART: GLEN KEANE. COPYRIGHT © 1982

**Animator Glen Keane drew this scene from "Mickey's Christmas Carol." What's his relationship to comics?**

FP-29: What was unusual about the villain who led the Monster Society of Evil against the original Captain Marvel?

FP-30: Who was Brick Bradford's main squeeze?

FP-31: Billy Batson became Captain Marvel by saying "Shazam!" What does Shazam stand for?

FP-32: How did Superman's pal Jimmy Olsen contact The Man of Steel?

FP-33: Which Marvel characters had their own comic strips?

FP-34: Name the founding members of The Avengers.

FP-35: How many members are there in the Green Lantern Corps?

FP-36: Which comic *book* creators worked on the *Star Trek* comic *strip*?

FP-37: Prof. Xavier runs what institution?

FP-38: What mysterious figure watched DC's heroes in 1983 and 1984?

FP-39: Marvel's first Captain Marvel came from what culture?

FP-40: Name Donald Duck's nephews.

FP-41: Which member of the *Star Wars* family was first introduced in the comic strip?

FP-42: How many novels were based on the *Star Hawks* strip?

FP-43: What team of comic artists produced the *Sky Masters* strip in the '50s?

FP-44: The characters in *Bloom County* think they are characters in what comic strip?

FP-45: When Batman's partner Robin takes off his mask tonight, who is he?

FP-46: If you invited the top crime fighter in Central City to dinner one night, who would show up at your door?

FP-47: What character was spun off into his own comic from Marvel's *2001* series?

FP-48: What do former Avengers Ant-Man, Giant-Man, Goliath and Yellowjacket have in common?

FP-49: What was Reuben Flagg's occupation before he became Plexus Ranger *American Flagg!?*

FP-50: The Fantastic Four has had more than four members in its history. Can you name all the heroes who have been part of this courageous quartet?

*(Answers appear on pages 191–93)*

# "V"— The Saga

V-1: What is the diameter of a mothership?

V-2: Around which star does the Visitor homeworld orbit?

V-3: What was Mike Donovan's profession before the invasion?

V-4: Name the actor who has played two roles on the series.

V-5: In which climate does the Red Dust not work?

V-6: Name Juliet Parrish's former lover who worked aboard the mothership, apparently as a collaborator.

V-7: Who is sacrificed during the Feast of Ramalon?

V-8: What is Lydia's rank?

V-9: What was the name of Donovan's wife?

V-10: Name Robin's younger sisters.

V-11: How long did the Red Dust antidote pills work?

V-12: Name the company headed by Nathan Bates.

V-13: For whom did Ham Tyler work prior to the invasion?

V-14: Which fantasy femme fatale portrayed a security commander during *The Final Battle*?

V-15: How did Elias die?

V-16: What is Chris' last name?

V-17: What makes Willie unique among his people?

V-18: In what special

solution do Visitors bathe their children?

V-19: Why did Charles want to marry Diana?

V-20: Who did Lydia and Diana frame for Charles' murder?

V-21: Which two women loved Kyle Bates?

V-22: What is the name of the religious leader among the Visitors?

V-23: What does Preta-na-ma mean?

V-24: Who hosted the Freedom Network news bulletins?

V-25: Who painted the first V?

"V" PHOTO: COPYRIGHT © 1984 WARNER BROS. INC.

**He blasted lizards into guacamole. Name the actor.**

*(Answers appear on pages 193–94)*

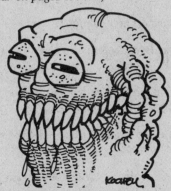

# Buck & Flash

BF-1: How many episodes were in the first Flash Gordon serial (1936)?

BF-2: What was Dr. Huer's (of the comic strip *Buck Rogers*) favorite thing to say?

BF-3: Who created Buck Rogers?

BF-4: In what century does Buck Rogers awaken?

BF-5: Who created Flash Gordon?

BF-6: Who was Buck Rogers' feathered friend on the recent TV series?

BF-7: Who were the favorite females, respectively, of Flash Gordon and Buck Rogers?

BF-8: What was the name of Buck Rogers' prototype shuttle in the recent TV series?

BF-9: On the TV series *Flash Gordon*, made in West

Germany in 1953, who portrayed that famed SF hero?

BF-10: Where did Buck Rogers *of the comics* sleep for 500 years?

BF-11: When Buck Rogers of the comics woke up after his snooze, who ruled the world?

BF-12: Who provided the original voice to Twiki on the *Buck Rogers* TV series?

BF-13: Who played Wilma Deering in the recent TV version of *Buck Rogers*—and who played her in the 1939 *Buck Rogers* serial?

BF-14: Buck Rogers' feathered TV pal is from what planet?

BF-15: In what century does Duck Dodgers awaken?

**Where did Flash Gordon and friends encounter the Clay Men?**

FLASH GORDON PHOTO: UNIVERSAL/CHARACTER COPYRIGHT KING FEATURES

BF-16: Who came first, Buck Rogers or Flash Gordon?

BF-17: What did Flash Gordon excell at before he went into space?

BF-18: When Buck Rogers was revived as a strip in the '70s, who illustrated it?

BF-19: Has Flash ever married Dale Arden in the comic strip?

BF-20: Who co-created *Get Smart* with Mel Brooks?

BF-21: Who did the score for the 1980 film *Flash Gordon*?

BF-22: Name two comic writers who wrote episodes of Buck Rogers. Name the episodes they wrote.

BF-23: In the film *Flash Gordon*, which important character was not represented properly?

BF-24: In the episode of *Buck Rogers* in which the Legion of Death appear, another SF hero's name is paged in a spaceport scene. Name him. Hint: he is a DC comics character.

BF-25: Why should Barry Allen and Wally West appear in this section?

*(Answers appear on pages 194–95)*

# The Bloody Pulps

BP-1: Give the nicknames of Doc Savage's assistants.

BP-2: Who wrote most of the pulp adventures of The Shadow?

BP-3: If you fought the Vampire Staffel, the Squadron of the Damned, and the Hurricane Patrol during World War I, you would be a member of what team?

BP-4: Who was the "Master of Men"?

BP-5: Why were pulps called pulps?

BP-6: Who was The Shadow, *really*?

BP-7: In what magazine might you find stories by Tennessee Williams, Robert E. Howard, Ray Bradbury and H.P. Lovecraft?

DOC SAVAGE PHOTO: COPYRIGHT © 1975 WARNER BROS. INC.

Doc Savage, Man of Bronze is in the middle. Director Michael Anderson is at left. But who's the legend wearing the cap and standing tall?

BP-8: Who were the pets of Monk Mayfair and Ham Brooks, respectively?

BP-9: Name The Shadow's main squeeze.

BP-10: Who wrote the adventures of Captain Future, Wizard of Science?

BP-11: What did Colonel John Renwick do to doors on a regular basis?

BP-12: Where did Doc Savage meet up with his team of assistants?

BP-13: Who is the Green Hornet's famous grand-uncle?

BP-14: Who knows what evil lurks in the hearts of men?

BP-15: What journalist (who worked at a trade magazine for undertakers) created Jules de Grandin and Dr. Trowbridge?

BP-16: Who wrote *Slan*?

BP-17: Who *really* wrote "Who Goes There?"

BP-18: In the film, who played the title role of *Doc Savage, The Man of Bronze*?

BP-19: Who has written "authorized" biographies of Tarzan and Doc Savage?

BP-20: Who was Adam Link?

BP-21: What piece of jewelry did The Shadow always wear?

BP-22: The Spider also carried a special symbol hidden on his person. What was it? And what did he use it for?

BP-23: In pulps, the "Man with a Thousand Faces" was a hero better known as . . . ?

BP-24: The most influential SF pulp began life under another title. What was it? And what was its later, more famed title?

BP-25: His hair is white. His face is waxy. And he fights evil aided by Justice, Inc. His name is . . . ?

*(Answers appear on pages 195–96)*

# Time Travel & Odysseys Two

TT-1: Name the stars of *The Time Tunnel*.

TT-2: What happened to the two American astronauts in the TV series *It's About Time*?

TT-3: *The Philadelphia Experiment* was an experiment in what?

TT-4: To what year does Christopher Reeve return *Somewhere in Time*?

TT-5: In the film *The Time Machine*, what was the *first* object to be sent into time?

TT-6: In *Time After Time*, what was the name of the H.G. Wells exhibit at the museum in San Francisco?

TT-7: In *Time After Time*, what year did H.G. Wells travel to?

TT-8: In what French SF film is a failed suicide asked to take part in a time travel experiment?

TT-9: If you owned John D. MacDonald's *The Gold Watch*, what could you do with it?

TT-10: In *The Terminator*, what must you wear outside your body while travelling through time?

TT-11: What is H.G. Wells' full name?

TT-12: In *2001*, what did the letters HAL stand for?

TT-13: Name the two actors who played Dr. Heywood Floyd.

TT-14: Who are the three active crew members on *Discovery 1*?

TT-15: On which airline did Dr. Heywood Floyd leave Earth?

TT-16: What did the Overlords in *Childhood's End* resemble?

**What are the occupations of those pictured?**

VOYAGERS PHOTO: COURTESY NBC.

TT-17: How did David Bowman's brother die?

TT-18: What happens to Jupiter in *2010*?

TT-19: What is the name of the Soviet spacecraft in *2010*?

TT-20: What is the main setting of Arthur C. Clarke's *The Fountains of Paradise*?

TT-21: What do the films *Close Encounters of the Third Kind*, *Altered States* and *2010* have in common?

TT-22: What film edged out *2001: A Space Odyssey* for a Best Screenplay Oscar?

TT-23: What was the original name of the Russian spaceship in *2010* (the book)?

TT-24: *2010* actors Elya Baskin, Oleg Rudnik and Savely Kamarov appeared in what other film together?

TT-25: Besides writing, what does Arthur C. Clarke do for a living?

*(Answers appear on pages 196–97)*

# Utopias & Distopias

UD-1: What did Charles Forbin create?

UD-2: Who was THX-1138's roommate?

UD-3: Where did Number Six reside?

UD-4: Peter Cushing, Edmund O'Brien and John Hurt. What role did they share?

UD-5: What is the meaning of Z.P.G.?

UD-6: Who wrote *Brave New World*?

UD-7: Who controls the world in the film *Rollerball*?

UD-8: In James Hilton's Shangri-La, what was the population of llamas and Tibetans?

UD-9: In Austin Tappin Wright's *Islandia*, how many foreigners can be in the country at one time?

UD-10: What is Jonathan E.'s number in *Rollerball*?

What might you call this utopia?

UD-11: What is the government known as in Howard Chaykin's *American Flagg!*?

UD-12: In futuristic films, Donald Pleasence, William Windom and John Ritter have all played what role?

UD-13: What does the original acronym EPCOT stand for?

UD-14: What is the name of the cure used on Alex in *A Clockwork Orange*?

UD-15: Who rules Shangri-La?

UD-16: Paul Newman plays a seal hunter in a derelict frozen city in what film?

UD-17: Name and differentiate the two planets that revolve around each other in Ursula K. LeGuin's *The Dispossessed*.

UD-18: Who is the protagonist in Austin Tappin Wright's *Islandia*? What is his position?

UD-19: At what temperature does paper burst into flames?

UD-20: What is moloko?

UD-21: In what year does the novel *Brave New World* open?

UD-22: If you were Winston Smith, what would you fear most?

UD-23: And if you were an inhabitant of Shangri-La, what might you consider the major benefit of living there?

UD-24: Who might you find on *The Road to Utopia*?

UD-25: Upon whose novel was the film *A Clockwork Orange* based?

*(Answers appear on pages 197–98)*

# Missions

M-1: In which film did Wolff and Niki attempt to rescue three women from the Forbidden Zone?

M-2: What spaceship did Leslie Nielsen command to Altair-4 in 2200 A.D.?

M-3: What was the name of the vessel which embarked on a *Fantastic Voyage*?

M-4: What did CMDF stand for?

M-5: Who were the three astronauts *Marooned*?

M-6: Who left Earth aboard *Capricorn One*?

M-7: If you were on the spaceship *Nostromo*, would you feel safe?

M-8: Why did Johnny Smith want to kill Greg Stillson?

M-9: In the world of *Fahrenheit 451*, what does a fireman do?

M-10: What sea-going mammal is, however improbably, involved in the mission undertaken in *Star Trek IV*?

M-11: Name the two spaceships in Disney's *The Black Hole*.

M-12: Who were the crew of *Capricorn One*?

M-13: What was *The Terminator*'s mission?

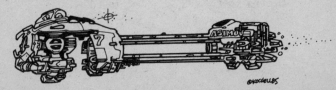

SALVAGE-1 PHOTO: COPYRIGHT UNIVERSAL TELEVISION

**Andy Griffith starred in *Salvage-1*. What was the name of his spaceship?**

M-14: How was the spaceship launched in *When Worlds Collide*?

M-15: In *Rocketship X-M*, what did X-M stand for?

M-16: What does Retief do for a living?

M-17: In Verne's *Master of the World*, what was Robur's goal?

M-18: Who conned a young hero into becoming *The Last Starfighter*?

M-19: How do you score in *Rollerball*?

M-20: What is the *Dark Star*'s mission?

M-21: What was Commando Cody's job?

M-22: What anti-gravity material was used for the trip in *The First Men in the Moon*?

M-23: Rex Reason visited the planet Metaluna in what film?

M-24: What type of vessel did Adam Quark (Richard Benjamin) command?

M-25: Who were "on a mission from God"?

*(Answers appear on pages 198–99)*

# Runners, Rebels, & Replicants

R-1: What's a blade runner's job?

R-2: What would you be if you were 31 in the world of *Logan's Run*?

R-3: What was the only way that a blade runner could distinguish a ''replicant'' from a human?

R-4: Who is the protagonist of *Blade Runner*?

R-5: What famed character actor did Arnold Schwarzenegger terminate early in *The Terminator*?

R-6: Upon what novel is *Blade Runner* based? Who wrote it?

R-7: Who is the leader of the renegade replicants in *Blade Runner*?

R-8: Who enters Manhattan in search of a

Below, on board *Blue Thunder* are Roy Scheider and JAFO Daniel Stern. What does JAFO mean?

BLUE THUNDER PHOTO: COPYRIGHT © 1983 COLUMBIA PICTURES

President in *Escape from New York*?

R-9: What company introduced what product in a commercial styled after George Orwell's vision of *1984*?

R-10: Where would you find a Spinner as a means of transport?

R-11: William F. Nolan and George Clayton Johnson created the mythos for what?

R-12: In *Black Sunday*, what is the occasion for an attempt on the life of the President?

R-13: What animal does Deckard's next door

*neighbor* own in the book upon which *Blade Runner* is based?

R-14: How is *The Terminator* destroyed?

R-15: If you drove a Landmaster, in what SF film would you be?

R-16: Would you find replicants in the book upon which *Blade Runner* is based?

R-17: Name the film nicknamed "High Noon in Space."

R-18: There are, thus far, three novel sequels to *Logan's Run*. What are they?

R-19: Tom Cody returned home to clean up the neighborhood and rescue former lover Ellen Aim in what film?

R-20: Robert Urich was a swashbuckling hero in which galactic turkey?

R-21: TV's John-Boy and the Man from U.N.C.L.E. traveled into outer space in this semi-famous SF film?

R-22: Who is The Firm's unofficial contact with *Airwolf*?

R-23: What was most remarkable (in a Hollywood movie buff-like way) about Yul Brynner's appearance in *Westworld*?

R-24: In what year is *Logan's Run* (film) set?

R-25: If you were being pursued by Jack McGee, who would you be?

*(Answers appear on pages 199–200)*

# Heavens Above, Hells Below

What hell did this heartless guy create for the President in *Dreamscape*?

DREAMSCAPE PHOTO: COPYRIGHT © 1983
CHEVY CHASE FILMS LIMITED PARTNERSHIP

H-1: What actor was used as a model for the Devil in the "Night on Bald Mountain" sequence in *Fantasia*?

H-2: Where did *The Greatest American Hero* get his powers?

H-3: What's Topper's problem?

H-4: What do Bill Cosby, George Burns, Peter Cook and Ray Walston have in common?

H-5: What were the different professions of Joe Pendelton in *Here Comes Mr. Jordan* and its remake, *Heaven Can Wait*?

H-6: What was David Niven's problem in *Stairway to Heaven*?

H-7: Poopdeck Pappy, Mr. Scratch, Mr. Hand and Luther Billis. What actor do these roles have in common?

H-8: In what film did Commander McHale join Captain Kirk to worship Satan?

H-9: Where did The Secret People of John Wyndham live?

H-10: What 18th Century English author predicted the existence of the two Martian moons?

H-11: What actress willingly receives the embraces of Ashtaroth in *To the Devil a Daughter* (1976)?

H-12: In the Arthur C. Clarke story, what happens after a computer finishes printing out ''The Nine Billion Names of God?''

H-13: Who supposedly wrote Norman Spinrad's SF novel *The Iron Dream*?

H-14: Who lives on Riverworld?

H-15: What SF book was Charles Manson enamored of?

H-16: Upon what does the house in *The Sentinel* sit?

H-17: In what household would you banter with such occasional visitors as Aunt Clara, Uncle Arthur and Abner Kravitz?

H-18: Richard Matheson scripted what 1972 TV movie?

H-19: What do Michael Landon, Henry Travers, Carl Reiner, Henry Jones and John Philip Law have in common?

H-20: Alan Alda tickled the ivories, becoming a concert pianist in what 1971 film?

H-21: If *Rosemary's Baby* didn't have a Devil for a dad, what actor would it call da-da?

H-22: To save the world and settle a bet between God and Satan, what did *Two of a Kind*, John Travolta and Olivia Newton-John, have to do in that 1983 movie?

H-23: Where would you find the names of *Satan's Cheerleaders*?

H-24: Vincent Price is noted for his many villainous roles, but only once did he play the ultimate villain—the Prince of Darkness, Satan—on the big screen. In what film?

H-25: Who is Daimon Hellstrom?

*(Answers appear on pages 200–01)*

# Spies & Intrigue

**SI-1:** Name the actors who have played James Bond.

**SI-2:** And name all the actors who have played M.

**SI-3:** What young actor had his first screen *leading* role in *Darby O'Gill and the Little People*?

**SI-4:** What film was remade into *Never Say Never Again*?

**SI-5:** What was The Prisoner's number?

**SI-6:** Leo G. Carroll portrayed what character in *The Man from U.N.C.L.E.* and *The Girl from U.N.C.L.E.*?

**SI-7:** What awakened Derek Flint from his death-like trances?

**SI-8:** In what film does James Bond appear in clownface?

**SI-9:** Who was *The Girl from U.N.C.L.E.*?

**What is the Fiendish Plot of Fu-Manchu?**

FU MANCHU PHOTO: COPYRIGHT © 1980 ORION PICTURES CORP.

**SI-10:** Whose *Licensed* (was) *Renewed* in John Gardner's novel?

**SI-11:** In *The Return of the*

Man from U.N.
C.L.E., who (actor-
wise) now heads
THRUSH?

SI-12: What were the
character names of
Diana Rigg and
Patrick Macnee in
*The Avengers*?

SI-13: Who is Modesty
Blaise's right-hand
man?

SI-14: They have both been
Matt Helm. Who are
they?

SI-15: What does U.N.
C.L.E. stand for?

SI-16: The IMF stands
for . . . ?

SI-17: And Marvel Comics'
spy group S.H.I.-
E.L.D. stands
for . . . ?

SI-18: If you were an agent
of the Probe Division
of World Securities,
what might you
carry—and where?

SI-19: How many Emmys
did Don Adams win
for his role in *Get
Smart*?

SI-20: In which films did
007 *personally* travel
into outer space?

SI-21: What is the name of
the superspy in *Cloak
and Dagger*? Who
played him?

SI-22: What three actors were the field operatives in TV's *Search*?

SI-23: Honor Blackman, Linda Thorson and Joanna Lumley all were paired with what character on television?

SI-24: What do you use to control the *Firefox*?

SI-25: What children's book did James Bond creator Ian Fleming write?

*(Answers appear on pages 201–02)*

# Scary Stuff

SS-1: What is the address of the Munsters?

SS-2: What H.P. Lovecraft story was adapted as *Die, Monster, Die*?

SS-3: Lon Chaney Jr., David Niven and John Carradine. All sunk their teeth into what role? And name the films.

SS-4: How did the Frankenstein Monster "perish" in the classic 1931 Universal film?

SS-5: Who portrayed Mary Shelley in *The Bride of Frankenstein*?

SS-6: What was peculiar about the town of *Salem's Lot*?

SS-7: What were the only distinguishable features of Cousin Itt in *The Addams Family*?

SS-8: The little girl menaced by *The Birds* grew up to be menaced by the *ALIEN*. Name her.

SS-9: What was the inspiration for the nasty creature in "The Crate," a segment of *Creepshow*?

SS-10: Who is "not like other boys?"

SS-11: What is "Redrum?"

SS-12: What model automobile was *Christine*?

SS-13: What was the name of the malevolent ventriloquist's dummy in *Magic*?

SS-14: Where is "the warmest place to hide?"

SS-15: In *Frankenstein Meets the Wolf Man* (1943), who played whom?

SS-16: In black & white, under what title would you find Marilyn, Eddie and Lilly?

SS-17: *The Addams Family* raised two kids. Name them.

SS-18: In the film *Carrie*, what single event sets Carrie to the mass destruction of her Senior Prom?

SS-19: If you want a drink at the bar in *The Shining* film, what bartender would you ask for?

SS-20: Who ''wouldn't hurt a fly'' in *Psycho*?

SS-21: According to H.P. Lovecraft, ''The Shadow is . . . ?

SS-22: At what resort might you stay in *The Shining*?

SS-23: In what film would you find the Chestburster?

SS-24: Who created the makeup for Boris Karloff's Frankenstein Monster?

SS-25: Who was the ''Man of a Thousand Faces''?

*(Answers appear on pages 202–03)*

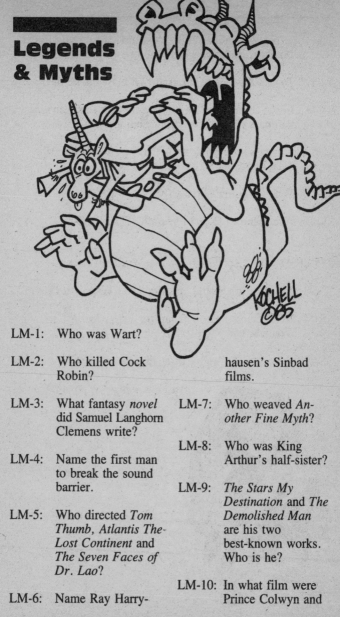

# Legends & Myths

**LM-1:** Who was Wart?

**LM-2:** Who killed Cock Robin?

**LM-3:** What fantasy *novel* did Samuel Langhorn Clemens write?

**LM-4:** Name the first man to break the sound barrier.

**LM-5:** Who directed *Tom Thumb, Atlantis The-Lost Continent* and *The Seven Faces of Dr. Lao?*

**LM-6:** Name Ray Harry-hausen's Sinbad films.

**LM-7:** Who weaved *Another Fine Myth?*

**LM-8:** Who was King Arthur's half-sister?

**LM-9:** *The Stars My Destination* and *The Demolished Man* are his two best-known works. Who is he?

**LM-10:** In what film were Prince Colwyn and

Princess Lyssa married?

LM-11: What will Peter Pan never do?

LM-12: The music of what composer was used to score the film *Excalibur*?

LM-13: What was the name of King Arthur's sword?

LM-14: Who directed *Woman in the Moon, M* and *Metropolis*?

LM-15: *Excalibur*'s John Boorman directed what 1977 horror film?

LM-16: Who was the author of *Frankenstein* married to?

**While Isabeau is a *Ladyhawke*, what is Navarre?**

LADYHAWK PHOTO: COPYRIGHT © 1984 WARNER BROS. INC. AND 20TH CENTURY FOX CORP

**LM-17:** If you were fated to be slain by a werewolf, what might it (or a fortune teller) see in your palm?

**LM-18:** What will happen to you if you gaze into the face of *The Gorgon* (1964)?

**LM-19:** What does a Scottish policeman find when he visits the island of *The Wicker Man*?

**LM-20:** George Lucas and George Miller have both cited one book as an inspiration and guide to myths they re-interpreted in their films. Name the book.

**LM-21:** Who gave King Arthur's sword to him?

**LM-22:** What actor/dancer was originally tapped for the role of the Tin Woodsman in *The Wizard of Oz*?

**LM-23:** Complete this couplet: "That is not dead, which may eternal lie . . ."

**LM-24:** What were the opening lines of *every* TV episode of *Star Trek*?

**LM-25:** Where would you find a Tarnsman?

*(Answers appear on pages 203–04)*

# Tarzans

T-1: Name Tarzan's ape mom.

T-2: Name the first and last Tarzan *novels* by Edgar Rice Burroughs.

T-3: Tarzan's chimp buddy has two different primary names (books and films). What are both?

T-4: The only writer to pen an authorized Tarzan novel beside Edgar Rice Burroughs is . . . ?

T-5: This actor portrayed the first Tarzan on the screen.

T-6: And this actor portrayed the latest?

T-7: What is the most remarkable fact about Tarzan as portrayed in the latest screen adaptation?

T-8: Several of the '30s/'40s Tarzan movies featured the apeman's adopted son. By what name is he called? What actor played him?

T-9: In Burroughs' novels, the apeman's son is not adopted, but his natural child. This character, featured prominently in *The Son of Tarzan*, is better known by what name? What is his christened name?

T-10: The Tarzan comic strip was illustrated for a time by Hal Foster (who would later create *Prince Valiant*). But another artist is best known as *the* Tarzan comic strip artist. Who is he?

T-11: Who is Tarzan's Oparian female friend?

T-12: In *Tarzan and the Golden Lion*, the apeman was portrayed by James Pierce. What was unusual about this?

T-13: The most well-known screen Jane married one of her Tarzan directors. Their daughter later carried *Rosemary's Baby*. Name all three.

T-14: On how many occasions did Johnny Weissmuller swing as Tarzan?

T-15: And in how many films did Buster Crabbe play the role?

T-16: In a famed spoof, what two TV comedians satirized Tarzan and Jane?

T-17: Tarzan rules a tribe of African natives. What is their name?

T-18: After Johnny Weissmuller left the Tarzan series, what African hero role did he assume in another movie series?

T-19: And after Weissmuller's young adopted son co-star left the Tarzan series, what jungle hero did he portray in yet another movie series?

T-20: Edgar Rice Burroughs worked in a California town. What is its name?

T-21: Why was the apeman such an enraged kind of guy in *Tarzan the Untamed*?

T-22: What is the name of Tarzan's Golden Lion?

T-23: After his victories, a 1970s Olympic swimming star announced he would never follow in the footsteps of his predecessors, Johnny Weissmuller and Buster Crabbe, and play Tarzan. Who is he?

T-24: In what Tarzan movie do we see a young James Bond?

T-25: How many Tarzan novels did Edgar Rice Burroughs write?

*(Answers appear on pages 204–05)*

**This triumphant apeman (Johnny Weissmuller) first swung across the screen in what year?**

TARZAN: JOHNNY WEISSMULLER/MGM/RKO

# Truly Bad Sci-Fi

TB-1: Who was *The Computer Wore Tennis Shoes*, and what college did he attend?

TB-2: What did Dr. Goldfoot's Bikini Machine do?

TB-3: What SF film is considered by many to be the *worst* film of all time?

TB-4: *I Was a Teenage Werewolf*. Who am I?

TB-5: What was "The Terror from Beyond Space?"

TB-6: Allison Hayes did what in 1958?

TB-7: Where was Flesh Gordon's muttering monster found?

TB-8: Nancy Sinatra appeared with Boris Karloff in this 1966 beach party movie.

TB-9: Why did *Mars Needs Women*?

TB-10: What "did in" *The Monolith Monsters*?

TB-11: What famous actress appeared (fully clothed) in *Santa Claus Conquers the Martians*?

TB-12: What actor paid a *Visit to A Small Planet* in 1960?

TB-13: What actor was Dr. Cyclops?

TB-14: And what could Dr. Cyclops do?

MEGAFORCE PHOTO: COPYRIGHT © 1982 NORTHSHORE INVESTMENTS LTD

**They probably wish they never made this movie. Who are they?**

TB-15: If you were Richard Jaeckel, what icky, gooey aliens would you be fighting in 1969?

TB-16: Who *Have Rocket, Will Travel*?

TB-17: Holy Rocket Crash! What former TV star bit the big one in *Robinson Crusoe on Mars*?

TB-18: *The Brain from Planet Arous* showcased a battle between two super-brains who had possessed the bodies of who?

TB-19: What SF film featured a Playboy Playmate of the Year later to be immortalized as Bob Fosse's *Star 80*? Who was she?

TB-20: Who were *The Far-Out Space Nuts*?

TB-21: Who was the *Queen of Outer Space*?

TB-22: What game did they play on the space base in *Moon Zero Two*?

TB-23: The aliens Fi and Fum on *The Lost Saucer* were . . . ?

TB-24: In one of his most unusual roles, he played an American journalist visiting the Captain Nemo of space. Name the actor and film.

TB-25: In what film would you find Commander Ace Hunter—*if* you wanted to find him?

*(Answers appear on pages 205–06)*

# The End of the World

EW-1: What three roles did Peter Sellers play in *Dr. Strangelove*?

EW-2: In what film will you find the *Space Ark*. And what was its destination?

EW-3: In *Space 1999*, on what date is the Moon blasted out of its orbit, and how?

EW-4: Upon what book was *Dr. Strangelove* based?

EW-5: What two heavenly bodies decided to mix it up in *When Worlds Collide*?

EW-6: Vincent Price and Charlton Heston played the lead role in movie versions of what Richard Matheson novel?

EW-7: In *End of the World* (1977), the aliens destroy Earth because we've been polluting all planets within light years with our diseases. Christopher Lee and fellow aliens masquerade as what while on Earth?

EW-8: In *Gas-s-s-s* (1970), who dies and how?

EW-9: These people saw their worlds end: Kal-El, Leia, Arthur Dent and Wonder Wart-Hog. Name the respective planets.

EW-10: How does Roland Young, *The Man Who Could Work Miracles*, almost end the world?

EW-11: Who rides the bomb down to Russia at the end of *Dr. Strangelove*?

EW-12: What two cities were destroyed in *Fail Safe*?

EW-13: What government agency unleashes ectoplasmic disaster upon New York in *Ghostbusters*?

EW-14: Why was the Earth destroyed in *The Hitchhiker's Guide to the Galaxy*?

EW-15: In *On the Beach*, where is the last outpost of humanity unaffected by radiation? Or—where's the beach?

EW-16: In which state does *Testament* take place?

EW-17: Who dies in *The 27th Day*?

EW-18: Who were the only three people left on Earth in *The World, the Flesh, and the Devil*?

EW-19: In what city is *The World, the Flesh, and the Devil* set?

EW-20: The nuclear destruction of which American city was featured in *The Day After*?

EW-21: In Clifford D. Simak's collection *City*, who inherits the Earth after mankind's departure?

EW-22: Who is the leader of the barbarian hordes in *The Road Warrior*?

EW-23: What destroys civilization in *Earth Abides* (by George R. Stewart)?

EW-24: What destroys civilization in *The Stand* (by Stephen King)?

EW-25: What happened when people watched *The Night of the Comet*?

*(Answers appear on pages 206–07)*

*A boy and His Dog.* Who voiced the Dog?

BOY AND HIS DOG PHOTO: COURTESY L.Q. JONES

# The Answers (No Peeking!)

## Cult Culture

*(Questions appear on pages 7–9)*

CC-1: Forrest J Ackerman.
CC-2: Santa Mira (1956)
and San Francisco (1978).
CC-3: *The Blob.*
CC-4: *Dallas* star Larry Hagman
directed *Beware the Blob.*
CC-5: David Bowie.
CC-6: Flubber.
CC-7: *Metropolis.*
CC-8: A shopping mall.
CC-9: The Positronic Ray.

METROPOLIS PHOTO: COURTESY NOVA

CC-10: Biblical plagues (rats, locusts, frogs, etc.).
CC-11: Droogs.
CC-12: Valentine Michael Smith.
CC-13: Induce orgasm.
CC-14: Dr. Lao, Pan, the Gorgon, Sorcerer, Apollonius,
the Abominable Snowman and the Sea Serpent.
CC-15: *Bwana Devil* (1952).
CC-16: To survive the race and score as many points as
possible by running over pedestrians. (Yes, really.)
CC-17: In and around Pittsburgh, Pennsylvania.
CC-18: *The Texas Chainsaw Massacre.*
CC-19: Ray Milland.
CC-20: *Return of the Fly* (1959) and *Curse of the Fly*
(1965).
CC-21: Gasoline.
CC-22: Frank Oz, of Miss Piggy and Fozzie the Bear fame,
mostly in cameo roles.
CC-23: Orson.
CC-24: Roman Polanski; Sharon Tate.
CC-25: 1) Sighting; 2) physical evidence; 3) contact of a
UFO. Only *you* can answer that second question.

## Today's Genre

*(Questions appear on pages 10–12)*

TG-1: As a child actor, Hunt portrayed the kid hero of the original (1953) *Invaders from Mars*. In a nostalgic casting move, he portrayed the police chief in the remake.

TG-2: 57 years.

TG-3: Writer Steve Gerber and artist Val Mayerik.

TG-4: Romance! Cherry 2000 is Sam's female robotic companion.

TG-5: Dr. Billy Hayes (Dean Paul Martin).

TG-6: He's a chimp!

TG-7: Majel Barrett and Jane Wyatt. Barrett, real-life wife of *Star Trek* creator Gene Roddenberry, portrays Dr. Christine Chapel, Spock's sometime love interest. Wyatt portrays Spock's mother, Amanda.

TG-8: Vincent Price.

TG-9: Number Five of *Short Circuit*.

TG-10: Heads up! Decapitation.

TG-11: Jones is a writer/performer member of the Monty Python comedy group. He directed a number of the group's films and has also written books of fairy tales for children.

TG-12: *Spies Like Us*.

TG-13: Charles Aidman. "And When the Sky Was Opened."

TG-14: Ridley Scott.

TG-15: *Flight of the Navigator*.

TG-16: You betcha! (Though many folks thought he was crazy.)

TG-17: Jennifer Connelly. David Bowie.

TG-18: In *Big Trouble in Little China*.

TG-19: *The Terminator*—which Cameron directed and in which Biehn and Henriksen starred.

TG-20: Actor Tim Curry.

TG-21: *King Kong Lives!*

TG-22: Goldblum's body has absorbed the fly's—which eventually takes over the scientist's human body, turning him into an insect-like monstrosity.

TG-23: Eddie Murphy.

TG-24: The barriers against evil are overturned and the encroaching darkness threatens to take over the whole world. (Moral: don't kill unicorns.)

TG-25: *Hyper Sapien.*

## Heroes & Heroines

*(Questions appear on pages 13–17)*

HH-1: Richard Coogan (1949–1950) and Al Hodge (1950–1956).

HH-2: He was an Independent News Service reporter who investigated unusual phenomena (*Kolchak: The Night Stalker*).

HH-3: Perry Rhodan.

HH-4: John Koenig and Dr. Helena Russell.

HH-5: *The Six Million Dollar Man.*

HH-6: Wonder Woman's chief squeeze.

HH-7: Perhaps the last survivor of the human race and leading character in *The Hitchhiker's Guide to the Galaxy.*

HH-8: According to confidential data, John Drake, the same as the *Secret Agent.*

HH-9: Captain Nemo.

HH-10: Christopher George.

HH-11: Captain Marvel (the character holds a remarkable resemblance to Fred MacMurray).

HH-12: Randy Claggett, Hickory Lee, Harry Jensen, Timothy Bell, Edward Cater and John Pope.

HH-13: He was a computer program.

HH-14: He took a government-produced super-power pill, good for one hour. Then, he was terrific.

HH-15: Alex Rogan (Lance Guest).

HH-16: Back off, men, they're *Ghostbusters.*

HH-17: Donald Duck.

HH-18: *Condorman.*

HH-19: *Wrong is Right* (Sean Connery plays Hale).

HH-20: Richard Crane.

HH-21: Nigel Kneale.

HH-22: Captain.

HH-23: Artemus Gordon, played by Ross Martin. (While Martin was ill—and off the show recuperating— actors William Schallert, Charles Aidman and Pat Paulsen substituted for him as other agents).

HH-24: Dick Tracy. The former two have played Tracy. Beatty may essay the role in a forthcoming film.

HH-25: Professor Bernard Quatermass.

HH-26: James Steranko, in production paintings for *Raiders of the Lost Ark*.

HH-27: A solar guard.

HH-28: Slippery Jim DiGriz.

HH-29: Elijah "Lije" Bailey.

HH-30: Sherlock Holmes. Woodward, of course, was his psychiatrist, Dr. Watson.

HH-31: Sir Arthur Conan Doyle.

HH-32: He had webbed fingers and toes.

HH-33: George Lucas' dog, Indy. (Arf! Arf!)

HH-34: *Barbarella*.

HH-35: Jenny Hayden.

HH-36: *Cyborg* by Martin Caidin.

HH-37: Office of Scientific Information (*The Six Million Dollar Man, The Bionic Woman*).

HH-38: Robby the Robot.

HH-39: Santa Claus.

HH-40: Alan Shepard.

HH-41: Raymond Burr.

HH-42: William Hartnell, Richard Hurndall (as a substitute for Hartnell), Patrick Troughton, Jon Pertwee, Tom Baker, Peter Davison, Colin Baker (all television); Peter Cushing (two films); Trevor Martin (stage).

HH-43: *One Million Years B.C.* (John Richardson and Raquel Welch, 1966).

HH-44: Superman.

HH-45: The Green Hornet. Bzzzz.

HH-46: Excalibur to King Arthur.

HH-47: Rick Deckard didn't know, but then who does? Rachael had *no* termination date.

HH-48: Sprog. (Seriously.)

HH-49: Captain America.

HH-50: "Buck."

# I, Robot

*(Questions appear on pages 18–23)*

R-1: Rosie (beep).

JETSONS PHOTO: COPYRIGHT © 1975
COLUMBIA PICTURES INDUSTRIES, INC.

R-2: Hank.

R-3: Julie Newmar (Rhonda the Robot).

R-4: Guardian.

R-5: Robert Vaughn (*Demon Seed*).

R-6: (1) A robot shall not injure a human, or, through inaction, allow harm to come to a human; (2) A robot shall obey the orders of a human unless such orders come into conflict with the First Law; (3) A robot shall protect itself from harm unless this conflicts with the First or Second Laws.

R-7: Isaac Asimov.

R-8: William Daniels.

R-9: Martin Caidin in his novel *Cyborg* (Kenneth Johnson adapted it for television).

R-10: Global Thermonuclear War.

R-11: *Android*.

R-12: The names of the two robots in love in *Heartbeeps*.

R-13: Tik-Tok.

R-14: Black Maria, a robotic replacement for the dissident Maria.

R-15: *Colossus* (1966), *The Fall of Colossus* (1974), and *Colossus and the Crab* (1977).

R-16: Questor. In *The Questor Tapes*, created by Gene Roddenberry.

R-17: Actor Dick Gautier.

R-18: Karel Capek in his 1921 stage play *R.U.R.*

R-19: Kirk Douglas straps dynamite to himself, and goes swimming with him. BOOM!

R-20: Ross Martin. A giant robot with the brain of a man.

R-21: It resembled a gorilla with a diving helmet.

R-22: Yoyo, as played by John Schuck (of *McMillan & Wife*).

R-23: Gigantor.

R-24: Dr. Coppelius.

R-25: Clickers.

## Fantasy Geography

*(Questions appear on pages 21–23)*

FG-1: Android spouses (*The Stepford Wives*).

FG-2: Tralfalmadore.
FG-3: The planet Mongo.
FG-4: Grover's Mills, New Jersey.
FG-5: Terminus.
FG-6: Fantasyland, Frontierland, Adventureland and Tomorrowland. (Other areas were added later.)
FG-7: The Earth's Core, according to Edgar Rice Burroughs.
FG-8: Skull and Manhattan.
FG-9: India.
FG-10: In a land called Honalee.
FG-11: Slumberland.
FG-12: Earth (also called Thulcandra).
FG-13: Perelandra, Malacandra, and Glundandra.
FG-14: Trantor.
FG-15: Mesklin.
FG-16: Pyrrus.
FG-17: Arrakis (or *Dune*).
FG-18: Planet 10 (*Buckaroo Banzai*).
FG-19: Devil's Tower.
FG-20: Saturn's third moon, Triton.
FG-21: Rama (*Rendevous with Rama*).
FG-22: Sogo.
FG-23: On a giant submarine under the sea.
FG-24: London.
FG-25: Zarathustra.

BUCKAROO BANZAI PHOTO:
COPYRIGHT © 1983 SHERWOOD
PRODUCTIONS, INC.

## Quotes

*(Questions appear on pages 24–25)*
Q-1: *Things to Come* (1936).
Q-2: The Monolith, *2010: Odyssey Two* (Arthur C. Clarke).
Q-3: Lord John Whorfin and his Red Lectroids, *The Adventures of Buckaroo Banzai—Across the Eighth Dimension*.
Q-4: Obi-Wan Kenobi (Alec Guinness) to Darth Vader in *Star Wars*.
Q-5: Carl Denham (Robert Armstrong) in *King Kong* (1933).

Q-6: The monster (Boris Karloff) in *The Bride of Frankenstein* (1935).

Q-7: The Robot in *Lost in Space*.

Q-8: Dr. Leonard McCoy (DeForest Kelley) "The Doomsday Machine."

Q-9: Dolphins, upon their departure from Earth in *The Hitchhiker's Guide to the Galaxy*.

Q-10: Opening sequence of *The Outer Limits*.

Q-11: Bill Murray to Sigourney Weaver in *Ghostbusters*.

Q-12: *The Prisoner*.

Q-13: *The Incredible Shrinking Man*, to the audience, as the film and he fade out.

Q-14: Daffy Duck, in the Warner Brothers cartoon.

Q-15: The creator (in the rabbit creation myth) in *Watership Down* by Richard Adams.

Q-16: David Bowman in *2001: A Space Odyssey*.

Q-17: *The Right Stuff*.

Q-18: Philip Nowlan's *Armageddon 2419 A.D.*, the first appearance of Buck Rogers.

Q-19: The opening line of Kurt Vonnegut's *Slaughterhouse-Five*.

Q-20: *The Abominable Dr. Phibes*.

Q-21: "Klaatu, barada nikto" (*The Day the Earth Stood Still*).

Q-22: Adam West, on TV's *Batman*.

Q-23: The Shadow.

Q-24: Jonathan Kent (Glenn Ford) to his son Clark (Jeff East) in *Superman*.

Q-25: Sean Connery as James Bond in *Goldfinger*.

## Boo! Hiss! (Villains!)

*(Questions appear on pages 26–31)*

BH-1: *The Invisible Man* (1931).

BH-2: Vincent Price (*Abbott and Costello Meet Frankenstein*). The boys met another invisible man (Arthur Franz) in a later film (1951).

BH-3: Sax Rohmer (Arthur Sarsfield).

BH-4: Too many. (We're not sure. Write and tell us.)

BH-5: *Dick Tracy* (1947).

BH-6: *The Man from Atlantis*; Victor Buono.
BH-7: Donald Pleasence (*You Only Live Twice*), Telly Savalas (*On Her Majesty's Secret Service*), Charles Gray (*Diamonds Are Forever*), and Max von Sydow (*Never Say Never Again*). Unidentified extras played his back and hands in other James Bond films. And that may or may *not* be Blofeld in *For Your Eyes Only*.
BH-8: Frank Gorshin and John Astin.
BH-9: Davros (*Doctor Who*).
BH-10: Black and Red Lectroids, from Planet 10.
BH-11: Eats them. Yum!
BH-12: Dr. Jekyll (and Mr. Hyde).
BH-13: Roddy McDowall (as Dr. Jonathan Willaway).
BH-14: Apokolips.
BH-15: Jonathan Harris.
BH-16: Cylons.
BH-17: Christopher Lloyd. (*Buckaroo Banzai, Star Trek III, Legend of the Lone Ranger* and *Taxi*).
BH-18: Dr. Yueh (Dean Stockwell).
BH-19: David Warner (*Time After Time, Time Bandits, The Man with Two Brains,* and *TRON*).
BH-20: David Cronenberg's *Scanners*.
BH-21: Hector. He was seven feet tall. You might call him, "Hector, *Sir*."
BH-22: Maximillian.
BH-23: Max von Sydow.
BH-24: In films, Lon Chaney Sr. (1925), Claude Rains (1940), and Herbert Lom (1960).
BH-25: Michael Dunn, *The Wild Wild West* (on the bottom half of the TV screen).
BH-26: To conceal a brutally disfigured face.
BH-27: The Mule (a.k.a. Maximus).
BH-28: Captain Video. (And his Video Rangers!)
BH-29: The diabolical Dragos.
BH-30: The MCP (Master Control Program).
BH-31: Peter Lorre as Le Chiffre.
BH-32: Flesh, human.
BH-33: Drive her crazy (and hush her up).
BH-34: They "drown" (but only until the next sequel).
BH-35: To steal away virile men to repopulate her planet. (Yes!!)

BH-36: No help from the audience please . . . Yes! 50 feet!

BH-37: Special Executive for Counterintelligence, Terror, Revenge and Extortion.

BH-38: An actor who played the Frankenstein Monster in several films (*House of Frankenstein*, *House of Dracula*, *Abbott & Costello Meet Frankenstein*). He later was a regular on *Gunsmoke* (as the bartender).

BH-39: The Bomb.

BH-40: Mrs. Deagle (Polly Holliday).

BH-41: That "Private Dancer" Tina Turner as Auntie Entity (*Mad Max Beyond Thunderdome*).

BH-42: Morgana LeFey.

BH-43: Felix the Cat.

BH-44: Dudley Dooright of the Royal Canadian Mounties (and his horse).

BH-45: Mr. Dark and his carnival.

BH-46: Underdog's nemesis.

BH-47: The Siren's deadly songs were aimed at *Batman*.

BH-48: Both are scientists working for the government who have a change of heart and decide to aid the hero.

BH-49: Fu Manchu.

BH-50: Bernie Kopell (KAOS mastermind Siegfried).

## Aliens & Other BEMs

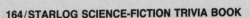

THE BROTHER FROM ANOTHER PLANET
PHOTO: COURTESY SEIFERT ASSOCIATES

*(Questions appear on pages 32–33)*

A-1: Jones.

A-2: Dan O'Bannon.

A-3: The head.

A-4: Ray Walston.

A-5: Frederic Brown.

A-6: Actor Harry Dean Stanton appears in all three.

A-7: M&Ms (*not* Reeses Pieces, as seen in the film).

A-8: *Lost in Space* and *Make Room for Daddy* (Angela Cartwright).

A-9: Mars. He was *My Favorite Martian*.

A-10: Just off Ellis Island.

A-11: H.R. Giger.

A-12: Quetzalchoatl, a winged serpent.

A-13: Sleep.
A-14: "Only a dream."
A-15: Martians (*Sherlock Holmes' War of the Worlds*).
A-16: They had disjointed pinky fingers.
A-17: Common Earth bacteria.
A-18: The monster from the id.
A-19: John Carpenter.
A-20: Bug-Eyed Monster.
A-21: Mercury Radio Theater, led by Orson Welles.
A-22: Quisp.
A-23: The Science Police.
A-24: The planet Mysteroid.
A-25: Monster Island.

## Epic Fiction

*(Questions appear on pages 34–36)*
EF-1: *Riverworld* by Philip José Farmer.
EF-2: September 22.
EF-3: Edward Stratemeyer and his Stratemeyer Syndicate. The books were written by many authors under the pseudonym Victor Appleton.
EF-4: Mott, Pope, Grant and Kolff.
EF-5: Isaac Asimov's Hari Seldon.
EF-6: Frodo Baggins, Sam Gamgee, Meriadoc Brandybuck, Peregrin Took, Gandalf the Grey, Boromir, Aragorn, Legolas the Elf and Gimli the Dwarf (*The Lord of the Rings*).
EF-7: *Foundation* (1951), *Foundation and Empire* (1952), *Second Foundation* (1953) and *Foundation's Edge* (1982).
EF-8: Four: North, South, East and West (*The Lord of the Rings*).
EF-9: Hanson's disease (leprosy).
EF-10: First Speaker, because in council, he spoke first.
EF-11: The Third Age.
EF-12: *Not for Hire* (also dubbed *Rex Grandissimus*, under the command of King John).
EF-13: Hama (*The Lord of the Rings*).
EF-14: Barsoom.

EF-15: Nine (*The Lord of the Rings*). (The real question is: how many can dance on the head of a pin?)
EF-16: South Africa.
EF-17: E.R. Eddison.
EF-18: The Old Forest (*The Lord of the Rings*).
EF-19: W.C. Fields.
EF-20: P.J. Travers.
EF-21: Deryni.
EF-22: Cimmeria.
EF-23: The Land.
EF-24: Brobdingnag.
EF-25: Valusia.

LORD PHOTO: COPYRIGHT © 1978 THE SAUL ZAENTZ PRODUCTION COMPANY

## Special Effects

*(Questions appear on pages 37–39)*

FX-1: "Seven skeletons fought three men," reveals Ray Harryhausen in his *Film Fantasy Scrapbook*, page 88, 1972 edition.
FX-2: The Zoptic Front Projection system, invented by Zoran Perisic.
FX-3: Red. Or Magenta. Or Pink. (That's the shade of it.)
FX-4: Introvision. The process creates the illusion that the actors are "in" rather than in front of a front projection plate.
FX-5: King Kong.
FX-6: *2001, Close Encounters, Blade Runner, Star Trek— The Motion Picture, Brainstorm, Ghostbusters, 2010.*
FX-7: Douglas Trumbull, Con Pederson, Tom Howard, Wally Veevers. Director Stanley Kubrick claimed credit for directing and designing the effects.
FX-8: *The Animal World*. A semi-documentary written, produced and directed by Irwin Allen. Willis O'Brien designed the dinosaurs and set-ups and Ray Harryhausen animated. The film was released in 1956 just two years before Harryhausen's super fantasy *The Seventh Voyage of Sinbad*.
FX-9: Joe Alves under the direction of Joshua Meador.
FX-10: *Gone With the Wind*. Among the old backlot sets burned for the destruction of Atlanta sequence was *King Kong's*.

FX-11: *Logan's Run.*

FX-12: *This Island Earth.* Faces turn purple during the trip to Metaluna.

FX-13: Three.

FX-14: *The Wizard of Oz. Poltergeist. Something Wicked This Way Comes. Country.*

FX-15: *ALIEN.*

FX-16: *Around the World in 80 Days.*

FX-17: *Invaders from Mars* (1953).

FX-18: James Arness.

FX-19: *When Worlds Collide* (1951).

FX-20: Magicam.

FX-21: *Earthquake, Rollercoster, Midway, Battlestar Galactica.*

FX-22: Rod Steiger in Bradbury's *The Illustrated Man.* According to the *Guinness book of Movie Facts and Feats:* Gordon Bau and his makeup crew of eight spent 10 hours completing the torso and another full day on the lower body hands and legs. (Notable runners-up include John Hurt for *The Elephant Man* and Lou Gossett for the Drac in *Enemy Mine.*)

FX-23: Spielberg's *Close Encounters of the Third Kind* shot its finale sequence inside an old blimp hangar in Alabama. The dimensions were 450 feet by 250 feet.

FX-24: William Tuttle in 1964 for *The Seven Faces of Dr. Lao,* and John Chambers in 1968 for *Planet of the Apes.*

FX-25: *Hollywood Boulevard* (1976), *Gremlins* (1984), *The Invisible Boy* (1957).

## Star Trek

*(Questions appear on pages 40–44)*

ST-1: Stun, kill, self-destruct and disintegrate solid objects.

ST-2: "Arena."

ST-3: NCC-1701/7; *Galileo.*

ST-4: Harcourt Fenton Mudd.

ST-5: David Gerrold.

ST-6: The Republic Pictures serial *Zombies of the Stratosphere*.

ST-7: Mark Lenard, as a Romulan commander in "Balance of Terror"; as a Vulcan, Sarek in "Journey to Babel," *The Voyage Home,* and *The Search for Spock*; and in a cameo as a Klingon in *Star Trek: The Motion Picture*.

ST-8: Yes, but a human cannot pronounce or typeset it.

ST-9: Two—"Assignment Earth" and "Tomorrow is Yesterday."

ST-10: Suspended animation ("Space Seed").

ST-11: Georgia, Earth.

ST-12: Gold—command; Blue—science; Red—engineering.

ST-13: Kirstie Alley (*Star Trek II: The Wrath of Khan*) and Robin Curtis (*Star Trek III: The Search for Spock*).

ST-14: Once every seven years.

ST-15: "Amazing Grace." The bagpipes.

ST-16: Christopher Pike ("The Cage"/"The Menagerie") and Robert April ("Counter-Clock Incident," animated *Trek*).

ST-17: Ann Crispin, in the *Star Trek* novel *Yesterday's Son*.

ST-18: Green.

ST-19: Bird of Prey (a title appropriated for the Klingon vessel in *Star Trek III: The Search for Spock*).

ST-20: On the bottom of the sleeve.

ST-21: Garland. It intersects Apollo Street.

ST-22: Dilithium crystals.

ST-23: Parents of Spock.

ST-24: Two—"Mudd's Women" and "I, Mudd."

ST-25: America. NBC. Thursday, 8:30–9:30 p.m.

ST-26: *U.S.S. Boobyprize*.

ST-27: The Tholians.

ST-28: Roger C. Carmel.

ST-29: Robert Bloch. "Catspaw," "Wolf in the Fold" and "What Are Little Girls Made Of?"

ST-30: Organia.

ST-31: Lt. Arex and Lt. M'ress.

ST-32: Half-Vulcan, half-Romulan.

ST-33: Kobyashai Muru (*Star Trek II: The Wrath of Khan*).

ST-34: Tribbles.

ST-35: Walter Koenig.

ST-36: D.C. Fontana and David Gerrold.
ST-37: David Gerrold and Howard Weinstein.
ST-38: "City on the Edge of Forever," Joan Collins; Lee Bergere, "All Our Yesterdays."
ST-39: They are on the back of the main saucer.
ST-40: John Belushi was Kirk; Chevy Chase, Spock; and Dan Akyroyd was both McCoy and Scotty.
ST-41: Three. Gold Key. Marvel Comics. DC Comics.
ST-42: *The Day the Earth Stood Still. The Andromeda Strain.*
ST-43: She was to be Spock's mate for "Amok Time."
ST-44: Gary Seven.
ST-45: Phasers and Photon Torpedoes.
ST-46: "The Changeling." "The Doomsday Device."
ST-47: No, they just met. (The film suggests differently.)
ST-48: Terri Garr as Miss Lincoln, Gary Seven's reluctant helper.
ST-49: That he was Scotty's nephew. This was acknowledged on the network TV premiere.
ST-50: T'Lar (Dame Judith Anderson).

# Teen Fantasies & Amazing Stuff

*(Questions appear on pages 45–47)*
TF-1: *D*ata *A*nalyzing *R*obot *Y*outh *L*ifeform. (Also the title of the movie.)
TF-2: In a high school gymnasium fighting for your life because *My Science Project* went wrong and created time warps which tend to import dinosaurs into our educational institutions.
TF-3: 1955 (*Back to the Future*).
TF-4: They targeted a laser on a new house and cooked up a homeful of hot buttered popcorn.
TF-5: Wak and Neek.
TF-6: An alien from Antares named Kitty in *Cocoon.*
TF-7: Mickey Mouse.
TF-8: That "Rathe" signed a hotel register book under a new but familiar name, Professor John Moriarty. Stay for credits and you learn loads!
TF-9: Amy Irving, Priscilla Pointer and Drew Barrymore have cameos in the "Ghost Train" episode. Irving is married to episode director Steven Spielberg.

Pointer, Irving's mother, is, natch, Spielberg's mother-in-law. Barrymore starred in the director's *E.T.*

TF-10: Actor Robert De Niro portrayed the renegade heating duct engineer.

TF-11: The Grateful Dead. Somehow appropriate.

TF-12: John Williams.

TF-13: It was an hour episode of *Amazing Stories*, but what's really amazing is that cartoon wheels showed up magically to save the poor bombardier who would have otherwise been severely crushed when the disabled plane landed. Gosh! Wow!

TF-14: *The Bride*. Crisp was the doctor helping Frankenstein (Sting) when he brought Eva (Jennifer Beals) to life.

TF-15: The 1931 *Frankenstein*—which they watched on TV ("colorized" from its original black & white)—not its sequel, *The Bride of Frankenstein* (sorry, Ernest Thesiger fans).

TF-16: Mariel Hemingway in *Creator*.

TF-17: Darren, portrayed by Jason Presson.

TF-18: The color purple, of course.

TF-19: *Brazil*.

TF-20: *The Clan of the Cave Bear*.

TF-21: Brontosaurus.

TF-22: Our *Lifeforce*!

TF-23: Mikey (Sean Astin), Chuck (Jeff B. Cohen), Data (Ke Huy Quan), Mouth (Corey Feldman), Stef (Martha Plimpton), Brand (Josh Brolin), Andi (Kerri Green) and Sloth (John Matuszak).

TF-24: Jim Henson's Creature Shoppe.

TF-25: Peter (Cushing) Vincent (Price).

## Ecology

*(Questions appear on pages 48–50)*

E-1: Food made from reprocessed, reconstituted people.

E-2: *Valley Forge*, Freeman Lowell. Earth's last forest.

E-3: Reptiles and amphibians in *Frogs*!

E-4: They are eight-inch-long black cockroaches which can set fire to people. They swarm out of a fissure in the

Earth's crust after an earthquake. They *laugh* at our puny roach motels!

E-5: Nuclear tests knock it out of orbit and send it careening towards the Sun.

E-6: A giant man-eating plant named Audrey Jr.

E-7: *Endangered Species*.

E-8: Dr. Moreau. Laughton—*Island of Lost Souls* (1933); Lancaster—*The Island of Dr. Moreau* (1977).

E-9: Salt water. (Moral: don't neglect your plants.)

E-10: Tana leaves.

E-11: They are transformed into beautiful queen bees, who love males to death (screenplay by Nicholas Meyer, in a weaker moment).

E-12: *The Creature from the Black Lagoon*.

E-13: Overpopulation.

E-14: Con-Amalgamated.

E-15: He grew to a height of 60 feet, terrorizing Las Vegas as *The Amazing Colossal Man*. Boy, was he big!

E-16: To increase productivity.

E-17: Alfred Krober.

E-18: Radium X.

E-19: An alien carrot (or plant life).

E-20: *Moby Dick*.

E-21: *Soylent Green*.

E-22: Huey, Dewey and Louie.

E-23: Upon its use, it freezes all the water on the Earth, and causes the end of the world, in Kurt Vonnegut's *Cat's Cradle*.

E-24: A Stillsuit (*Dune*). (Or you would be in big trouble—since it retains all the bodily moisture you need to survive.)

E-25: Rendering planets habitable for humans, a term coined by Jack Williamson.

## Bizarre Stuff

*(Questions appear on pages 51–53)*

BS-1: Captain Video used it on his enemies. It vibrated them to death. Yow!

BS-2: Hitler, Albert Einstein, Mozart, Lewis Carroll, Jack

the Ripper, Walt Disney and Jesus Christ, among others (*Happy Birthday, Wanda June*).

BS-3: It is a computer that rapes her (*Demon Seed*).

BS-4: *The Wizard of Oz*.

BS-5: The answer to the question, "What is the meaning of life?" in *The Hitchhiker's Guide to the Galaxy*.

BS-6: Jesus Christ in *Jesus on Mars*.

BS-7: He smiles too much. (But does he "have a nice day?") Actually, his facial muscles have been paralyzed into a sardonic grin.

BS-8: *See You Next Wednesday*. (You can see posters advertising it and other references to it in Landis' films.)

BS-9: *The Unseen Hand* by Sam Shepard.

BS-10: *Gremlins*.

BS-11: *Shock Treatment*.

BS-12: Heads blowing up.

BS-13: She (Mariette Hartley) had two belly buttons.

BS-14: Sex outside of one's species. (Or at least that's what he calls it.)

BS-15: Mike Todd Jr., for the film *The Scent of Mystery*.

BS-16: 99 cards, 22 stickers.

BS-17: On the back of a giant moth. (True!)

BS-18: It's a giant egg hatched by the Sun.

BS-19: He was an alien robot.

BS-20: Four per green Martian.

BS-21: For creating a Pink Bunkadoo (a terribly tall & ugly tree).

BS-22: "Oonie-oops."

BS-23: He swallowed a pill that made him hiccup 100 times, then explode. Some fun, eh? But don't try this at home.

BS-24: Benny Hill. Ian Fleming (of 007 fame) wrote the book.

BS-25: Sweden, Norway and Finland.

## Sword & Sorcery

*(Questions appear on pages 54–56)*

SO-1: *Wizards and Warriors*.

SO-2: Robert E. Howard.

SO-3: Gary Gygax.

SO-4: Robert E. Howard. (Again!)

SO-5: *Pumping Iron*, a movie about musclemen (though Schwarzenegger made a barely released film before it, as "Arnold Strong" in *Hercules in New York*).

SO-6: Jack Kirby.

SO-7: John Norman's Gor series.

SO-8: Anne McCaffrey's Dragonrider series.

SO-9: Fritz Leiber.

SO-10: She's a swordswoman.

SO-11: The Hyborean Age.

SO-12: Very pale (he's an albino).

SO-13: Sanctuary.

CONAN PHOTO: COPYRIGHT © 1984
UNIVERSAL CITY STUDIOS/DINO
DE LAURENTIIS CORP.

SO-14: Elric. (And Red Sonja in her film).

SO-15: Frodo Baggins (*Lord of the Rings*).

SO-16: Thulsa Doom (portrayed in *Conan the Barbarian* by James Earl Jones).

SO-17: L. Sprague de Camp, Lin Carter, Bjorn Nyberg, Karl Edward Wagner, Andrew J. Offutt, Poul Anderson, Catherine Crook de Camp and "Robert Jordan" (in Lancer, Ace, Bantam and Tor paperback editions). Several other writers are now working on new Conan novels.

SO-18: Miaowara Tomokato. He's *Samurai Cat*!

SO-19: Lin Carter. All three are paperback series—in the tradition of Howard and Burroughs—penned by Carter.

SO-20: Dave Sim, comics artist/writer. His character is Cerebus, a barbarian aardvark.

SO-21: Cija—Jane Gaskell; Brak—John Jakes; Kane—Karl Edward Wagner; Solomon Kane—Robert E. Howard; Kothar—Gardner Fox; Hawkmoon—Michael Moorcock.

SO-22: The Bicentennial Series (*The Bastard, The Rebels,* etc.), celebrating American history. Several of the volumes were adapted as TV mini-series.

SO-23: Strange.

SO-24: Elric, Dorian Hawkmoon, Erikose, Prince Corum, Jerik Carnelian, Jerry Cornelius.

SO-25: Thoth-Amon.

# Star Wars

*(Questions appear on pages 57–61)*

SW-1: Tuskan raiders.

SW-2: Tatooine.

SW-3: Twin Ion Engine.

SW-4: Interpretation and protocol.

SW-5: May 25, 1977.

SW-6: Peter Mayhew, a.k.a. Chewbacca.

SW-7: Leigh Brackett. She also co-wrote *The Empire Strikes Back*.

SW-8: Carbonite.

SW-9: Boba Fett. Jeremy Bulloch.

SW-10: *Amadeus*. The title role, Wolfgang Amadeus Mozart. (Hamill also appeared on Broadway in *The Elephant Man* and *Harrigan and Hart*.)

SW-11: Wickett.

SW-12: H. Beam Piper's Fuzzies and Gordon Dickson and Poul Anderson's Hokas.

SW-13: NPR—National Public Radio.

SW-14: 66 cards, 11 stickers. (Now, *that's* trivia!)

SW-15: Dagobah.

SW-16: Aunt Beru and Uncle Owen.

SW-17: Roy Thomas, who co-storied *Conan the Destroyer*, wrote it and *American Flagg!* creator Howard Chaykin drew it.

SW-18: Biggs Darklighter.

SW-19: C-3PO and R2-D2, Luke Skywalker (as a hologram), Han Solo (in carbonite), Chewbacca and Princess Leia (disguised as a bounty hunter), Lando Calrissian (as one of Jabba's guards), Han Solo (de-freezed), and Luke (in the flesh).

SW-20: Han Solo opens up a tauntaun with the sabre to save Luke's life in the second reel of the 70mm *Empire Strikes Back*.

SW-21: That Chewbacca has a wife and kid who live with Chewie's paw (father).

SW-22: "Aren't you a little short for a stormtrooper?"

SW-23: Charles Martin Smith and Richard Dreyfuss.

SW-24: Nope. In *Star Wars*, he destroyed Alderaan despite his bargain with Leia.

SW-25: *A New Hope*

SW-26: Lando Calrissian.

SW-27: Anakin Skywalker.

SW-28: Tatooine has two suns and thus, two sunsets.

SW-29: Dantooine.

SW-30: Dark Lord of the Sith.

SW-31: Master Yoda (John Lithgow).

SW-32: 3,720 to one, but don't tell a Corellian the odds.

SW-33: Docking bay 94.

SW-34: Han Solo.

SW-35: Wedge Antilles (Denis Lawson).

SW-36: Obi-Wan Kenobi.

SW-37: Industrial Light & Magic.

SW-38: The *Devastator*.

SW-39: Julian Glover was General Veers in *Empire* and Kristatos in *For Your Eyes Only*.

SW-40: David Prowse as the bodyguard to the old man Malcolm McDowell assaulted.

SW-41: *Blue Harvest*.

SW-42: His death.

SW-43: A *Star Wars* bed sheet, action figures, Chewbacca jacket, Darth Vader poster and a blaster.

SW-44: Luke as they approached the Death Star. Leia in *Empire*. C-3PO and Han in *Jedi*.

SW-45: *Flash Gordon*.

SW-46: Steven Spielberg. The Indiana Jones adventures.

SW-47: A bellhop in *Dead Heat on a Merry-Go-Round*. He was told by producers that he would never make it in the business.

SW-48: *Lost in Space. The Time Tunnel. Land of the Giants*.

SW-49: Harrison Ford.

SW-50: "May the Force be with you."

# Irwin Allen Fun

*(Questions appear on pages 62–64)*

IA-1: *Jupiter 2*.

IA-2: Kurt Kasznar.

IA-3: The *Seaview*.

IA-4: Zachary, you bubble-headed booby (*Lost in Space*).

IA-5: Admiral Harriman Nelson (*Voyage to the Bottom of the Sea*, film and TV).

IA-6: The Communists.

IA-7: *Spindrift*.

IA-8: Model B-9, an environmental control robot.

IA-9: The *Sea Crab* and the *Flying Fish*.

IA-10: Dick Tufeld. Bob May.

IA-11: Captain Lee Crane, portrayed by David (Al) Hedison.

IA-12: Zorro. Black.

IA-13: Professor John Robinson, Major Don West, Maureen Robinson, Judy Robinson, Penny Robinson, Will Robinson, and the Robot (Dr. Smith was an unwilling stowaway).

IA-14: They all have music composed by John Williams.

IA-15: Jonathan Harris.

IA-16: *Land of the Giants* takes place in 1983 and the Robinsons got lost in 1997.

IA-17: London.

IA-18: David Hedison, of course. He appears in both—as Captain Lee Crane and as CIA agent Felix Leiter.

IA-19: The *Titanic*.

IA-20: *Voyage to the Bottom of the Sea*.

IA-21: *The Twilight Zone*. He appeared in "It's a Good Life," "Long Distance Call" and "In Praise of Pip."

IA-22: June Lockhart lost her daughter Anne to *Galactica 1980*.

IA-23: Jonathan Harris.

IA-24: Chariot.

IA-25: Captain Lee Crane (David Hedison). (OK, we *like* David Hedison questions—he's a nice guy.)

## Apes & Primates

*(Questions appear on pages 65–67)*

AP-1: Rod Serling and Michael Wilson.

AP-2: The Alpha-Omega Bomb, a nuclear device.

AP-3: Pierre Boulle. *Monkey Planet*.

AP-4: John W. Chambers.

AP-5: The man-ape who touches the Monolith and changes his destiny in *2001: A Space Odyssey*.

AP-6: "Murders in the Rue Morgue."
AP-7: Ken Russell's *Altered States*—it's William Hurt regressing.
AP-8: Gorilla Grodd.
AP-9: Paparazzi (and their photo flashes).
AP-10: To clothe King Kong (primarily the large models) for the classic's filming.
AP-11: Barbra Streisand. (Really!)
AP-12: Cornelius and Caesar—father and son (films) and Galen (TV).
AP-13: Military.
AP-14: Orangutans and chimpanzees.
AP-15: Konga (1961).
AP-16: Soror.
AP-17: Wolves.
AP-18: Max Steiner.
AP-19: The Ogrons.
AP-20: Mark Lenard.
AP-21: A night club.

KING KONG ESCAPES PHOTO: COPYRIGHT © 1968 UNIVERSAL PICTURES

AP-22: Banana peels. (Director John Landis wore the costume.)
AP-23: He played an ape named Dino.
AP-24: Sydney in *The Incredible Shrinking Woman*.
AP-25: Depends on where you live. Prints released in America featured the ape's victory, but the version shown in Japan boasted a winning Godzilla.

## SF Women

*(Questions appear on pages 68–69)*
W-1: Jaime Sommers (Lindsay Wagner).
W-2: Catwoman (TV's *Batman*).
W-3: Caroline Munro.
W-4: Madison, after the avenue.
W-5: Start fires by mind powers.
W-6: She was injured sky diving, and endowed with bionic legs, one bionic arm and a bionic ear.
W-7: Phoebe Cates (*Gremlins*). (And that's why she hates Christmas!)

W-8: *Thunderball* and its remake *Never Say Never Again*.
W-9: Helen Slater.
W-10: Adrienne Barbeau.
W-11: *Cat People*.
W-12: Maya (*Space: 1999*)
W-13: ESP. (Yes, that's all).
W-14: Paradise Island.
W-15: Sybil Danning.
W-16: Ursula K. LeGuin.
W-17: Ming the Merciless.
W-18: Ayesha (H. Rider Haggard's *She*).
W-19: Shirley Temple.
W-20: Brigitte Nielsen.
W-21: Morrill.
W-22: Fairuza Balk.
W-23: Elsa Lanchester.
W-24: *Fantastic Voyage* (small) and *One Million Years B.C.* (prehistoric).
W-25: Anne Francis.

## The Doctor

*(Questions appear on pages 70–73)*
D-1: John Leeson and David Brierly.
D-2: Time and Relative Dimensions in Space.
D-3: Sydney Newman and Donald Wilson.
D-4: "Arc of Infinity."
D-5: United Nations Intelligence Taskforce.
D-6: Alistair.
D-7: Metebelis 3 (a.k.a. "Planet of Spiders").
D-8: Liz Shaw.
D-9: To marry Professor Clifford Jones.
D-10: Barry Letts (seasons 7 through 12).
D-11: Harry Sullivan. Ian Marter.
D-12: The Cybermen.
D-13: Terry Nation.
D-14: Ray Cusick.
D-15: Susan Foreman, Ian Chesterton and Barbara Wright.
D-16: Dido.
D-17: Sara Kingdom ("The Dalek Masterplan").

D-18: Mavic Chen, Guardian of the Solar System.
D-19: Turlough (Mark Strickson). The Black Guardian.
D-20: The Wirrn.
D-21: Mutts.
D-22: The recorder.
D-23: Cybermats.
D-24: The Sontarans.
D-25: Linx, ''The Time Warrior.''
D-26: The Ice Warriors.
D-27: Trisilicate.
D-28: Aggedor.
D-29: Jelly babies.
D-30: Gold.
D-31: Voga.
D-32: Vortis.

DR. WHO PHOTO: COPYRIGHT © 1981 BBC TV

D-33: The Zarbi, the Menoptera, and Animus.
D-34: Journalist.
D-35: *Curse of the Daleks.*
D-36: Roger Delgado, Peter Pratt, Geoffrey Beevers and Anthony Ainley.
D-37: Verity Lambert.
D-38: The Zygons.
D-39: The Krynoid.
D-40: Matthew Waterhouse.
D-41: As an award for mathematic excellence.
D-42: ''Earthshock,'' part four.
D-43: The credits were run in silence over a closeup of Adric's shattered badge.
D-44: Ron Grainer.
D-45: ''An Unearthly Child,'' ''The Tribe of Gum.''
D-46: ''The Tenth Planet,'' The First Doctor (William Hartnell) regenerates into the Second Doctor (Patrick Troughton).
D-47: Mondas and Telos.
D-48: Queen Thalira.
D-49: ''Shada.''
D-50: *Doctor Who Meets Scratchman.*

## Funny Stuff

*(Questions appear on pages 74–76)*
FS-1:  Flesh Gordon.
FS-2:  *Sleeper* (1973).
FS-3:  Douglas Adams.
FS-4:  Commander Link Hogthrob, Dr. Strangepork, and Miss Piggy—they are *Pigs in SPAAAAAACE*!
FS-5:  The *Heart of Gold* (*The Hitchhiker's Guide to the Galaxy*).
FS-6:  Buck Henry.
FS-7:  *Jews in Space*.
FS-8:  Steven Spielberg, as a government clerk.
FS-9:  Splat!!! (The poor deer gets squashed)
FS-10: The Stay-Puft Marshmallow Man.
FS-11: William Daniels.
FS-12: Author Stephen King (who scripted the film).
FS-13: Aluminum foil. (It's a wrap!)
FS-14: George Fenneman and *The Thing* (1952).
FS-15: *Heartbeeps*.
FS-16: *The Brother from Another Planet*.
FS-17: *Airplane II—The Sequel*.
FS-18: *Penthouse*.
FS-19: *Slapstick* by Kurt Vonnegut.
FS-20: *The Mouse on the Moon*.
FS-21: He was paranoid and *extremely* depressed (*The Hitchhiker's Guide to the Galaxy*).
FS-22: Don Knotts.
FS-23: A pack of cigarettes (tar).
FS-24: Terry Gilliam.
FS-25: The Leader's *nose*, the only surviving portion of him after an assassination attempt.

## Battlestar Galactica

*(Questions appear on pages 77–79)*
BG-1:  Muffit II.
BG-2:  ''Damn!'' (There are *other* words.)
BG-3:  A centon.
BG-4:  Colonel Tigh (played by Terry Carter).

BG-5: 17.
BG-6: Sunday, ABC (8 p.m. E.S.T.).
BG-7: Captain and Lieutenant.
BG-8: Glen Larson.
BG-9: Serina, a Caprican newswoman.
BG-10: She was a sociolater, *Galactica* terminology for prostitute.
BG-11: Borellians.
BG-12: Lloyd Bridges.
BG-13: Greenbean.
BG-14: Blue Squadron. Sheba.
BG-15: *Magnum P.I., Tales of the Gold Monkey* and *Airwolf.*
BG-16: *Vipers.*
BG-17: 12, one for each of the ancient races of humanity.
BG-18: Serina (Jane Seymour), Boxey's mother.
BG-19: Baltar, traitor of mankind.
BG-20: Fred Astaire.
BG-21: Three. (That may also be how many it takes to change a light bulb.)
BG-22: Reptiles.
BG-23: Two—*Galactica* and *Pegasus.*
BG-24: The Universal Studios tour, where the aliens attacked tourist trams.
BG-25: John Colicos. He was Baltar and a *Star Trek* Klingon Kor ("Errand of Mercy).

# Oscars & Honors

*(Questions appear on pages 80–82)*
O-1: Leopold Stokowski and Walt Disney.
O-2: Hugo Gernsback, famous SF editor.
O-3: Ridley Scott.
O-4: Peter Ellenshaw (*The Black Hole, 20,000 Leagues Under the Sea, Mary Poppins*).
O-5: The Neil Armstrong Air and Space Museum.
O-6: Best new SF writer of the year.
O-7: Stanley Kubrick, *Dr. Strangelove, 2001: A Space Odyssey* and *A Clockwork Orange.*

O-8: *The Twilight Zone* (1960, 1961, 1962).

O-9: Hugo, Nebula, Galaxy, Jupiter, John W. Campbell and International Fantasy.

O-10: Ursula K. LeGuin, for *The Left Hand of Darkness* and *The Dispossessed*.

O-11: *The Forever War*.

O-12: Rick Baker, *An American Werewolf in London* (1981).

O-13: Santa Claus in *Miracle on 34th Street*. Ho-ho-ho.

O-14: *Rosemary's Baby*.

O-15: "Best Moon Landing Ever." (Really!)

O-16: Sound effects (*Goldfinger*).

O-17: *King Kong* (effects by Carlo Rambaldi, Glen Robinson and Frank Van der Veer).

O-18: False. Only *Star Wars* was nominated (and lost to Woody Allen's *Annie Hall*).

O-19: Seven: Art Direction, Costume Design, Editing, Sound, Visual Effects, Original Score and a Special Award (for robot voices).

O-20: It's non-existent. No awards were given that year.

O-21: True.

O-22: Soundtrack veteran Jerry Goldsmith.

O-23: Six: Les Bowie, Colin Chilvers, Dennys Coop, Roy Field, Derek Meddings and Zoran Perisic.

O-24: They all won Oscars for Best Editing.

O-25: Harlan Ellison, *The Starlost* (the actual program carried a pseudonymous credit).

## The Written Word

*(Questions appear on pages 83–88)*

WW-1: Ira Levin.

WW-2: Miniaturization.

WW-3: George Orwell. It's his real name, Orwell was a pseudonym.

WW-4: Norman Bean (a typo of *Normal* Bean—since the author wanted people to know he wasn't crazy). Appeared later as *A Princess of Mars* by Edgar Rice Burroughs.

WW-5: Lazarus Long.

WW-6: Kill off Captain Kirk. "He's dead, Harlan."

WW-7: Kilgore Trout, a fictional creation of Kurt Vonnegut. Philip José Farmer later wrote a book also entitled *Venus on the Half-Shell* under the pseudonym Kilgore Trout.

WW-8: Robert Heinlein.

WW-9: Sydney Aaron (aka Paddy Chayefsky).

WW-10: Charles Beaumont.

WW-11: Poul Anderson.

WW-12: Gregory Benford. *Timescape*.

WW-13: Ben Bova.

WW-14: Talbot Mundy.

WW-15: To preserve the works of H.P. Lovecraft and other *Weird Tales* authors in hardback form.

WW-16: E.E. ''Doc'' Smith.

WW-17: Robert Silverberg.

WW-18: Germany.

WW-19: *Stephen King's Danse Macabre*. (Sorry, the other books are *not* true stories).

WW-20: *Space Cadet* by Robert Heinlein.

WW-21: *Gladiator* (1930).

WW-22: John F. Kennedy; Ian Fleming's James Bond.

WW-23: Harlan Ellison.

WW-24: Via the wardrobe.

WW-25: Rudyard Kipling, Selma Lagerlof, Maurice Maeterlinck, Anatole France, Vladislav Reymont, George Bernard Shaw, Thomas Mann, Sinclair Lewis, Herman Hesse, Bertrand Russell, Winston Churchill, John Steinbeck, Jean Paul Sartre, Harry Martinson and Isaac Bashevis Singer. (Real hard, isn't it?)

WW-26: Winston Churchill.

WW-27: *The Dragon in the Sea* (also known as *Under Pressure*).

WW-28: Xanth.

WW-29: *A Canticle for Leibowitz*.

WW-30: Zenna Henderson.

WW-31: Fred Hoyle's *The Black Cloud*.

WW-32: L. Ron Hubbard.

WW-33: Lewis Carroll.

WW-34: *The Gods Themselves*.

WW-35: Olaf Stapledon.

WW-36: An SF fan group in the 1940s, whose members encouraged each other to write. Alumni include Frederik Pohl, Isaac Asimov, James Blish and others.
WW-37: Philip Wylie.
WW-38: *Fahrenheit 451* and *Something Wicked This Way Comes*. (Several other films have been based on various Bradbury short stories.)
WW-39: *Travels into Several Remote Nations of the World by Lemuel Gulliver, First a Surgeon, then a Captain of Several Ships* (1726), by Jonathan Swift.
WW-40: Michael Crichton.
WW-41: "Who Goes There?" by Don A. Stuart.
WW-42: *The Modern Prometheus*.
WW-43: Lyman.
WW-44: Stephen King. Bachman is a pseudonym.
WW-45: *Titan, Wizard* and *Demon*.
WW-46: The Empire State Building.
WW-47: *The Birth of the People's Republic of Antarctica* (1983).
WW-48: The Castle of the House of Groan.
WW-49: "Repent, Harlequin."
WW-50: Jeff Rice.

## Twilight Zone

*(Questions appear on pages 89–91)*
TZ-1: Friday (10–10:30)
TZ-2: "Nothing in the Dark" (Robert Redford, later the Sundance Kid, was the actor).
TZ-3: Burgess Meredith, "Time Enough at Last."
TZ-4: "Nightmare at 20,000 Feet" (Nick Cravat, who plays the Gremlin).
TZ-5: Rod Serling's English teacher/mentor.
TZ-6: Born in Syracuse, NY—grew up in Binghamton, NY.
TZ-7: A dinosaur and the Trylon and Perisphere of the 1939 New York World's Fair.
TZ-8: 1959, on CBS.
TZ-9: "A Nice Place to Visit" (Sebastian Cabot).

TZ-10: "Night of the Meek" (Art Carney).

TZ-11: A devil's head.

TZ-12: Abraham Lincoln.

TZ-13: *The Waltons* (Earl Hamner Jr.)

TZ-14: Two tiny men.

TZ-15: Disguises himself as a robot boxer and fights a robot opponent.

TZ-16: Martian three, Venusian three ("Will the Real Martian Please Stand Up?").

TZ-17: She makes a "Long Distance Call" via toy telephone.

TZ-18: Nikita Khruschev ("The Whole Truth").

TZ-19: To stall Mr. Death from taking a child.

TZ-20: Cookbooks and gourmet food.

TZ-21: The ability to foretell who would die in battle.

TZ-22: "I Sing the Body Electric" (scripted by Bradbury).

TZ-23: A department store mannequin.

TZ-24: A hanging.

TZ-25: "Kick the Can," "It's a Good Life" and "Nightmare at 20,000 Feet."

## Classics

*(Questions appear on pages 92–94)*

C-1: The *Albatross*.

C-2: *Forbidden Planet*.

C-3: Four (Jacob Marley's ghost, Christmas Past, Christmas Present, and Christmas Yet-to-Come).

C-4: Fortunato, for the love of God!

C-5: Jacob and Wilhelm. They *did* smile occasionally.

C-6: Ichabod Crane.

C-7: *The Day the Earth Stood Still*. Gort, the robot.

C-8: An aging portrait of himself. It gets older; he stays young.

C-9: *Five Weeks in a Balloon*.

C-10: Roald Dahl, Patricia Neal, and *The Day the Earth Stood Still*. (Dahl and Neal have since divorced.)

C-11: *The Hunchback of Notre Dame*.

C-12: Sam Jaffe.

C-13: Georges Melies.

C-14: "Atom powered."

C-15: *A Trip to the Moon* (1902).

C-16: *Nosferatu* (1922).

C-17: *The Incredible Shrinking Man* (1957).

C-18: France.

C-19: *Forbidden Planet*.

C-20: Kevin McCarthy and Dana Wynter. (And Larry Gates, King Donovan, Carolyn Jones, Virginia Christine, Whit Bissell, and Richard Deacon.)

C-21: Natalie Wood. She didn't believe in Santa Claus.

C-22: The late Francois Truffaut.

C-23: William Shakespeare.

C-24: They abandon their balloon during a hurricane—but it's a different balloon than the *Five Weeks in a Balloon* trip.

C-25: Douglas Trumbull.

## Songs & Sounds

*(Questions appear on pages 95–97)*

SO-01 God in the 1950 film.

SO-02: He comes and beats the living daylights out of you (*The Second Chronicles of Thomas Covenant*).

SO-03: Bernard Herrman.

SO-04: Hoyt Axton is a successful country singer-songwriter (as well as actor).

SO-05: The late Ted Cassidy (who also did the opening voiceover). You know him better as Lurch on *The Addams Family*.

SO-06: Comedian Howie Mandel (Dr. Wayne Fiscus on *St. Elsewhere*).

SO-07: Deborah Harry.

SO-08: John Williams. Again!

SO-09: Jerry Goldsmith.

SO-10: Rysling, jetman of the Goshawk.

SO-11: *Alfred Hitchcock Presents*.

SO-12: *Star Trek*.

SO-13: High frequency sound.

SO-14: "In the Year 2525."

SO-15: Pink Floyd.

SO-16: Elton John ("Rocket Man").

SO-17: "Human Touch."
SO-18: They are the same person—Carlos underwent a sex change.
SO-19: John Philip Sousa. (His work was adapted for the film by Frank De Vol.)
SO-20: "Singin' in the Rain."
SO-21: Smoke cigars.
SO-22: Supreme Headquarters Alien Defense Organization (*UFO*).
SO-23: You take a jump to the left, then a step to the right. Put your hands on your hips and pull your knees in tight. But it's the pelvic thrust that really drives you insane. Let's do the Time Warp again. (Say, does anyone here know how to Madison?)
SO-24: The planet Transsexual (in the galaxy of Transylvania).
SO-25: "Don't dream it, be it."

BUGS BUNNY PHOTO: COPYRIGHT WARNER BROS. INC.

## Animations of Life

*(Questions appear on pages 98–102)*
AL-1: Jan, Jace and Blip.
AL-2: Colonel Steve Zodiac.
AL-3: Dr. Boynton's wife and son had been killed in an automobile accident. He built Astro Boy as a companion.
AL-4: *Supercar* (1959, TV).
AL-5: "A secret compartment of my ring I fill/With an Underdog Super Energy Pill."
AL-6: *The Wonderful Worlds of the Brothers Grimm.*
AL-7: Gary Owens.
AL-8: *Pinocchio in Outer Space.*
AL-9: Ymir (or "Ymir, Sir").
AL-10: Max and Dave Fleischer (animation pioneers—Popeye, Superman and Betty Boop). They're his father and uncle, respectively.
AL-11: *Star Trek.*
AL-12: *The Dark Crystal* (1982).
AL-13: Bud Collyer.
AL-14: Elias.

AL-15: Doc, Happy, Grumpy, Sneezy, Sleepy, Bashful and Dopey. (Other versions of the fairy tale sometimes feature dwarfs with other names.)

AL-16: World Aquanaut Security Patrol (Gerry Anderson's *Stingray*).

AL-17: The Great Gazoo, Harvey Korman.

AL-18: Spacely Space Sprockets.

AL-19: Old Nazi propaganda films.

AL-20: The kindly wizard blew away the evil wizard with a Luger. Could it be magic?

AL-21: Dodo, the Kid from Outer Space.

AL-22: *Space Angel* (sorry—*Clutch Cargo* wasn't really SF).

AL-23: *He-Man*.

AL-24: Purple (*The Sword and the Stone*).

AL-25: National Institute of Mental Health.

AL-26: Johnny Quest.

AL-27: *Dragon's Lair* and *Space Ace*.

AL-28: Cogswell, of Cogswell Cogs.

AL-29: "So Beautiful, So Dangerous," "Taarna," "Soft Landing," "Captain Sternn," "B-17," "Harry Canyon" and "Den."

AL-30: Pokey. Orange.

AL-31: The Fooderackacycle.

AL-32: The Traffic Zone.

AL-33: Buzz Conroy.

AL-34: Dr. Zinn.

AL-35: He chewed Oxygum.

AL-36: He-Man.

AL-37: *G.I. Joe*.

AL-38: *Gigantor*.

AL-39: Spectrum, on *Captain Scarlet*.

AL-40: *Thunderbirds*.

AL-41: *Yamato*.

AL-42: Tobor, a powerful robot.

AL-43: *Rabbit Fire* (1951), *Rabbit Seasoning* (1952) and *Duck Rabbit Duck* (1953).

AL-44: Frostbite Falls, USA.

AL-45: Wotsamatta U.—on a football scholarship, no less!

AL-46: Both feature a villain named Riff Raff.

AL-47: Robin, the Boy Wonder (Kasem also voiced

Shaggy on *Scooby Doo* and Mark on *Battle of the Planets*, among others).

AL-48: *Captain Harlock.*

AL-49: That "*Mighty Mouse* in on the way," of course.

AL-50: Mark Hamill. (Whatever happened to him?)

# SF TV

*(Questions appear on pages 103–105)*

SF-1: Dumont (1949–1956).

SF-2: Interstellar terrorist or freedom-fighter, depending upon whom you talked to.

SF-3: David McCallum (*The Invisible Man*) and Ben Murphy (*The Gemini Man*). (Ghosts are another story, sorry.)

SF-4: Simon Jones.

SF-5: Richard Anderson (as Oscar Goldman on *The Six Million Dollar Man*, ABC, and *The Bionic Woman* on ABC and later, NBC).

SF-6: *The Starlost* (Bird is a pseudonym for Harlan Ellison).

SF-7: The alien spaceship used by Roj Blake in *Blake's Seven* to fight the Federation.

SF-8: In *Space: 1999* (as well as on the Moon).

SF-9: The robot companion played by Donald Moffat in the *Logan's Run* TV series.

SF-10: He gets white-eyed and green-skinned, and beats up bad guys as *The Incredible Hulk*.

SF-11: *Disneyland* (as the TV series was then known).

SF-12: *The Man from Atlantis.*

SF-13: Moonbase Alpha (*Space: 1999*).

SF-14: School teacher and FBI agent.

SF-15: *Space Journey: 1999.*

SF-16: Barney Miller (*not* the TV cop), played by Monte Markham in *The Six Million Dollar Man*.

SF-17: *A Tales of Tomorrow* episode entitled "Ice from Space." He was paid $164 for a week's work.

SF-18: *Space Patrol.*

SF-19: Dick York and Dick Sargent.

SF-20: Telepaths from another dimension, as played by Joanna Lumley and David McCallum in the British TV series.

SF-21: The Bermuda Triangle.
SF-22: Inside the Great Pyramid at Cheops.
SF-23: Three: CBS, ABC and NBC.
SF-24: United Planets of the Universe (TV's *Space Patrol*).
SF-25: Don Herbert.

## Wondrous Worlds

*(Questions appear on pages 106–108)*

WO-1: Selenites.
WO-2: Somewhere *20,000 Leagues Under the Sea*.
WO-3: *Saint-Michel*.
WO-4: *The Last Starfighter*.
WO-5: Gaia.
WO-6: Large variable-speed moving belts known as the Roads.
WO-7: *The Dark Crystal*.
WO-8: *E.T.*
WO-9: Dexter/Ace, Kimberly and the evil Borf.
WO-10: *Out of the Silent Planet, Perelandra* and *That Hideous Strength*.
WO-11: Gelfling.
WO-12: Greg and Tim.
WO-13: Pinky, Inky, Blinky and Clyde.
WO-14: *WARP*.
WO-15: Caspak. It's on the island of Caprona in the South Pacific.
WO-16: The asteroid belt.
WO-17: The Frankenstein Monster, Count Dracula, the Wolf Man, the Mad Doctor and the Hunchback.
WO-18: Mars.
WO-19: John Ronald Reuel.
WO-20: Talos.
WO-21: A. Merritt.
WO-22: Silver. (They were, of course, changed to ruby slippers for the MGM film.)
WO-23: Rukbat.
WO-24: *The Dark Crystal* (1982).
WO-25: *Westworld, Futureworld* and *Beyond Westworld*.

## Giant or Otherwise Unusual Animals

*(Questions appear on pages 109–110)*

G-1: A six-foot-tall invisible rabbit (pooka), and best friend of Jimmy Stewart.

G-2: Eight, plus two lengthy feeler-tentacles.

G-3: Penguins. They were animated. He wasn't.

G-4: Sir Arthur Conan Doyle.

G-5: Radioactive mutant giant ants.

G-6: Giant killer bunnies.

G-7: Expose him to bright light, get him wet, or feed him after midnight.

G-8: *The Fly* and *The Satan Bug*.

G-9: The special FX wizard who designed the *Gremlins*.

G-10: *Five*. Ray Harryhausen reduced the number of tentacles to save time and money.

G-11: Pigs.

G-12: *Kingdom of the Spiders*.

G-13: *Gremlins*.

G-14: Algernon, a white mouse (*Charly, Flowers for Algernon*).

G-15: Daggits.

G-16: Bruce Mattey.

G-17: Pushme-pullyu and Pollynesia.

G-18: Zunar 5J/90 Doric Fourseven.

G-19: Pern. (And of course they ride *dragons*).

G-20: *Gammera The Invincible* (1966).

G-21: Grasshoppers.

G-22: Smash *The Fly* with a rock before a spider eats him.

G-23: Cockroaches. Yuk.

G-24: Godzooke (in the Saturday morning cartoons) and Minilla (in the movies).

G-25: Awful music.

## See You in the Funny Papers

*(Questions appear on pages 111–115)*

FP-1: Kirk Alyn, George Reeves and Christopher Reeve.

FP-2: Alley Oop.

FP-3: Gotham City (The Joker in *Batman*).

FP-4: Forms of Kryptonite and magic.

FP-5: "In brightest day, in blackest night, no evil shall escape my sight. Let those who worship evil's might, beware my power—Green Lantern's light!"

FP-6: General Zod, Ursa and Non.

FP-7: Carl Barks.

FP-8: Hippolyta, Queen of the Amazons.

FP-9: He loses his powers.

FP-10: Yes, she's his cousin Kara.

FP-11: Judge Dredd.

FP-12: Ron Goulart and Gil Kane.

FP-13: Zeta Beam.

FP-14: He doesn't. He is seen *only* as a poster on the wall of her room, and is briefly mentioned on the radio and in other lines of dialogue.

FP-15: Mariette Hartley, in an Emmy-winning role.

FP-16: John Coleman Burroughs, the author's son.

FP-17: *The Black Hole*. (He also did *2001*—but that's not a 1979 SF film).

FP-18: Jerry Siegel and Joe Shuster (1938).

FP-19: "Spa fon!" and "Squa tront!"

FP-20: Kal-El of Krypton. Clark Kent is his *adopted* Earth name.

FP-21: Sweethaven.

FP-22: *The Time Top*.

FP-23: Dan Dare.

FP-24: Planets.

FP-25: The Silver Surfer.

FP-26: Ray Bradbury.

FP-27: Cathy Lee Crosby (in a 1974 TV movie pilot).

FP-28: ABC *and* CBS.

FP-29: The insidious genius, Mr. Mind, was a worm (we mean a *real* worm).

FP-30: Saturn Sadie.

FP-31: Wisdom of Solomon, strength of Hercules, stamina of Atlas, power of Zeus, courage of Achilles, and speed of Mercury.

FP-32: A signal watch that only Superman could hear ("zee zee zee").

FP-33: Spider Man, the Incredible Hulk, Conan the Barbarian and Howard the Duck.

FP-34: Hulk, Thor, Iron Man, Ant-Man and the Wasp.

FP-35: 3600.

FP-36: Gerry Conway and Ernie Colon.

FP-37: The School for Gifted Students.

FP-38: The Monitor.

FP-39: The war-like Kree.

FP-40: Huey, Dewey and Louie.

FP-41: Admiral Ackbar.

FP-42: Two, both by Ron Goulart.

FP-43: Jack Kirby and Wally Wood.

FP-44: *Star Trek* (with disabled vet Cutter John and his wheelchair acting as Kirk and the *Enterprise*, respectively).

FP-45: Bruce Wayne's adopted son, Jason Todd. (Dick Grayson, the original Robin, is now Nightwing, leader of *The New Teen Titans*.)

FP-46: Better set an extra place. Both the Spirit (by Will Eisner) and the Earth-One Flash beat up baddies in cities named Central.

FP-47: *Machine Man* (introduced as X-51).

FP-48: They are all identities assumed at various times by Dr. Henry Pym.

FP-49: He starred in a soft-core video show as *Mark Thrust, Sexus Ranger* (until he was replaced by a computer-generated holographic image of himself).

FP-50: Mr. Fantastic, The Thing, Invisible Girl, The Human Torch, Crystal, Medusa and Power Man all have been official members while Tigra, Thundra, the Black Panther, Wyatt Wingfoot and the Impossible Man get involved in occasional adventures. Alicia Masters might also be considered a member. Add the She-Hulk to the still-growing (over the years) list of official members.

## "V"—The Saga

*(Questions appear on pages 116–117)*

V-1: Five miles.

V-2: Sirius.

V-3: Photo-journalist—TV.

V-4: Frank Ashmore as Martin and Philip.
V-5: Warm climates.
V-6: Dr. Steven Maitland.
V-7: The youngest warrior or youngest fleet officer.
V-8: Adjutant.
V-9: Marjorie.
V-10: Polly and Katie.
V-11: 24 hours.
V-12: Science Frontiers.
V-13: The Firm a.k.a. the CIA.
V-14: Sarah Douglas.

"V" PHOTO: NBC/WARNER BROS. TV

V-15: He was killed by a Visitor ray gun blast.
V-16: Faber.
V-17: He is a vegetarian.
V-18: Rock salt and machine oil.
V-19: It was a scheme to send her home, leaving command to himself and his lover Lydia.
V-20: Marta, the chemist.
V-21: Robin Maxwell and Elizabeth Maxwell.
V-22: Zon.
V-23: Peace.
V-24: Howard K. Smith.
V-25: Abraham Bernstein.

## Buck & Flash

*(Questions appear on pages 118–20)*

BF-1: 13
BF-2: "Heh!"
BF-3: Philip Nowlan, in the short story "Armageddon 2419."
BF-4: 25th.
BF-5: Alex Raymond.
BF-6: Hawk (portrayed by Thom Christopher).
BF-7: Dale Arden and Wilma Deering.
BF-8: *The Ranger*.
BF-9: Steve Holland, later an artist's model for paperback covers, including those of Doc Savage by James Bama.

BF-10: In a cave.
BF-11: Mongolians.
BF-12: Mel Blanc, of Bugs Bunny and Barney Rubble fame.
BF-13: Erin Gray and Constance Moore.
BF-14: Throm.
BF-15: The 24th and a half.
BF-16: Buck Rogers.
BF-17: Football.
BF-18: Gray Morrow.
BF-19: No, not yet.
BF-20: Would you believe, Buck Henry?
BF-21: Rock group Queen.
BF-22: Alan Brennert: "Plot to Kill a City." "Comic Wiz Kid." Marty Pasko: "Happy Birthday, Buck."
BF-23: Thom, the Lion Man.
BF-24: Adam Strange.
BF-25: Because they are the Flash and Kid Flash, respectively. That's why.

## The Bloody Pulps

*(Questions appear on pages 121–23)*
BP-1: Monk, Ham, Renny, Long Tom and Johnny.
BP-2: Walter B. Gibson (as Maxwell Grant).
BP-3: G-8 and his Battle Aces.
BP-4: The Spider.
BP-5: They were printed on extremely cheap pulpwood paper.
BP-6: Pilot Kent Allard—though he also adopted the identity of wealthy man about town Lamont Cranston and is best known to many fans under that alter-ego.
BP-7: *Weird Tales.*
BP-8: Habeas Corpus (a pig) and Chemistry (an ape).
BP-9: Margo Lane (no relation to Lois—unless you ask Philip José Farmer).
BP-10: Edmond Hamilton.
BP-11: Knock the panels out of them with his large fists.
BP-12: In a prisoner of war camp during World War I.
BP-13: The Lone Ranger.
BP-14: The Shadow knows. Moo hya hya hya hya!

BP-15: Seabury Quinn.
BP-16: A.E. Van Vogt.
BP-17: John W. Campbell, under the pseudonym Don A. Stuart.
BP-18: Ron Ely.
BP-19: Philip José Farmer.
BP-20: A robot appearing in stories by Eando (Otto) Binder.
BP-21: A fire opal ring.
BP-22: A cigarette lighter whose base hid a special stamp. The Spider used it to stamp his mark—a red spider—on the foreheads of the criminals he killed.
BP-23: Secret Agent X, his nickname derived from his ability at disguise. (On occasion, The Avenger was also referred to by the same nickname.)
BP-24: *Astounding Stories*. It later became *Analog*— and is still being published today under that title.
BP-25: Richard Benson, The Avenger. (He's one of the few pulp heroes to have *new* adventures written about him—by Ron Goulart as "Kenneth Robeson" —when the originals, then being reprinted by Warner Books, had all been republished).

## Time Travel & Odysseys Two

*(Questions appear on pages 124–26)*

TT-1: James Darren and Robert Colbert. Lee Meriwether and Whit Bissell also starred.
TT-2: They went through a time warp and ended up in the Stone Age. (Later in the series, they returned to Earth, changing the format, bringing Stone Age folks to present-day Earth.)
TT-3: Radar invisibility. It went awry, and ended up in a time travel problem.
TT-4: 1912.
TT-5: A cigar.
TT-6: "H.G. Wells: A Man Before His Time."
TT-7: 1979.
TT-8: Alain Resnais' *Je t'aime, Je t'aime*.
TT-9: Speed up time.

TT-10: Nothing but your birthday suit.
TT-11: Herbert George Wells.
TT-12: *H*euristic *AL*gorithmic (*not*, as was popularly believed, to be "just one step ahead of IBM").
TT-13: William Sylvester (*2001: A Space Odyssey*) and Roy Scheider (*2010*).
TT-14: Frank Poole, David Bowman and the HAL 9000.
TT-15: Pan Am.
TT-16: Devils.
TT-17: In a drowning accident.
TT-18: It becomes a small sun.
TT-19: *Leonov*.
TT-20: Sri Lanka.
TT-21: Actor Bob Balaban has major roles in all three.
TT-22: Mel Brooks' *The Producers*.
TT-23: *Cosmonaut Gherman Titov*.
TT-24: *Moscow on the Hudson*.
TT-25: He is Chancellor of the University of Moraturwa, near Colombo, Sri Lanka.

## Utopias & Distopias

*(Questions appear on pages 127–29)*
UD-1:  Colossus, the U.S. defense supercomputer.
UD-2:  ŁUH-3417.
UD-3:  The Village (in *The Prisoner*).
UD-4:  Winston Smith in *1984*. (Cushing, British TV; O'Brien & Hurt, film versions).
UD-5:  Zero Population Growth.
UD-6:  Aldous Huxley.
UD-7:  Several large corporations.
UD-8:  50 llamas, 1000 Tibetans.
UD-9:  100.
UD-10: Six.
UD-11: The Plex.

A CLOCKWORK ORANGE PHOTO: COPYRIGHT © 1971 WARNER BROS.

UD-12: The President of the United States (*Escape from New York*, *Escape from Planet of the Apes* and *Americathon*).
UD-13: Experimental Prototype Community of Tomorrow.

UD-14: Ludivico-Technique, a kind of Shock-Center-Aversion Therapy.

UD-15: The High Lama.

UD-16: *Quintet* (1979).

UD-17: Urras, rich and fertile; and Anneras, barren and poor.

UD-18: John Lang, American counsel to Islandia.

UD-19: *Fahrenheit 451*.

UD-20: Milk with drugs in it (*A Clockwork Orange*).

UD-21: Year After Ford 632.

UD-22: Rats (*1984*).

UD-23: That you could live "forever" in peace and happiness (*Lost Horizon*).

UD-24: Bing Crosby, Bob Hope and, of course, Dorothy Lamour (1945).

UD-25: Anthony Burgess'.

## Missions

*(Questions appear on pages 130–32)*

M-1: *Spacehunter*.

M-2: Relief Saucer C57D.

M-3: The *Proteus*.

M-4: Combined Miniature Deterrent Forces (*Fantastic Voyage*).

M-5: Richard Crenna, James Franciscus and Gene Hackman.

M-6: Nobody. The mission to Mars was faked (according to the movie).

M-7: No, because no one in space can hear you scream (*ALIEN*).

M-8: He foresaw Stillson as becoming the U.S. president who would start World War III (*The Dead Zone*).

M-9: Burn books.

M-10: Whales.

M-11: *Cygnus* and *Palomino*.

M-12: O.J. Simpson, Sam Waterston and James Brolin.

M-13: To terminate Sara Connor.

M-14: It was launched on a long, curved ramp on railway tracks.

M-15: Expedition Moon.

M-16: He's an intergalactic diplomat in a series of novels by Keith Laumer.

M-17: To destroy all instruments of war.

M-18: Centauri, as played by Robert Preston.

M-19: Get the large metal ball into the goal and hurt as many people on the way as you possibly can.

M-20: To destroy unstable planets.

M-21: He was a Sky Marshal, tracking interstellar criminals.

M-22: Cavorite.

M-23: *This Island Earth*.

M-24: An interplanetary garbage scow.

M-25: The Blues Brothers—Jake and Elwood. Of course!

## Runners, Rebels, & Replicants

*(Questions appear on pages 133–35)*

R-1: Search and "retire" renegade artificial humans.

R-2: Dead, or running. No one is permitted to live beyond the age of 30.

R-3: A complex series of tests using retinal scanning and verbal interrogation to determine their incapacity for compassion/empathy.

R-4: Rick Deckard.

R-5: Dick Miller.

R-6: *Do Androids Dream of Electric Sheep*? by Philip K. Dick.

R-7: Roy Batty, played by Rutger Hauer.

R-8: Snake Plissken, played by Kurt Russell.

R-9: Apple Computer and their Macintosh. The commercial was directed by *Blade Runner*'s Ridley Scott.

R-10: *Blade Runner*, of course (not *The Moon-Spinners*, not *Spin & Marty*).

R-11: *Logan's Run*.

R-12: The Super Bowl.

R-13: A horse. (*Neigh*bor—get it? It was a hint.)

R-14: Shot, run over by a truck, burned beyond recognition, blown up, and crushed. "Takes a licking, but keeps on ticking!"

R-15: *Damnation Alley* (also known as *Survival Run*).

R-16: No. They are called *androids* in the book.
R-17: *Outland.*
R-18: *Logan's Search, Logan's World* (both by Nolan), *Jessica's World* (by Johnson).
R-19: *Streets of Fire.*
R-20: *Ice Pirates.*
R-21: *Battle Beyond the Stars.*
R-22: Michael Archangel (actor Alex Cord).
R-23: He wore the same black gunfighter's outfit he had worn as Chris, gunfighter leader of *The Magnificent Seven* (1960) and *Return of the Seven* (1966).
R-24: 2074.
R-25: David Banner, *The Incredible Hulk* (of TV).

## Heavens Above, Hells Below

*(Questions appear on pages 136–38)*
H-1: Bela Lugosi.
H-2: Through a red suit given to him by aliens.
H-3: His best friends (Marion and George Kirby) and their dog are dead, and haunting him.
H-4: They have all played the Devil. Cosby—*The Devil and Max Devlin* (1981); Burns—*Oh God, You Devil* (1984); Cook—*Bedazzled* (1967); and Walston—*Damn Yankees* (1958).
H-5: Boxing and football—but both played the saxophone.
H-6: He was scheduled to be killed, in a plane crash, but due to a heavenly goof-up, survived (and then fell in love).
H-7: Ray Walston.
H-8: *The Devil's Rain* (starring Ernest Borgnine and William Shatner).
H-9: Under the Sahara.
H-10: Jonathan Swift.
H-11: Nastassja Kinski.
H-12: One by one, the stars go out.
H-13: Adolph Hitler.
H-14: The 36,006,009,637 men, women, and children who dwelt on Earth during the first several million years of human existence until 1983.

H-15: Heinlein's *Stranger in a Strange Land*—particularly the passages concerning cannibalism.
H-16: The gateway . . . to HELL!
H-17: The Stevens household in *Bewitched*.
H-18: *The Night Strangler* (Matheson's two 1971 TV movies were *Duel* and *The Night Stalker*).
H-19: They're all angels! Landon—*Highway to Heaven*; Travers—*It's a Wonderful Life*; Reiner—*Good Heavens*; Jones—"Mr. Bevis" on *Twilight Zone*; and Law—*Barbarella*.
H-20: *The Mephisto Waltz*.
H-21: John Cassavetes.
H-22: Fall in love (which they had plenty of practice doing in *Grease*).
H-23: Across their chests (on their tee-shirts).
H-24: Irwin Allen's *The Story of Mankind* (1957).
H-25: The Son of Satan, one of Marvel Comics' *Defenders*.

## Spies & Intrigue

*(Questions appear on pages 139–41)*
SI-1: Barry Nelson (TV); David Niven, Woody Allen, Peter Sellers (*Casino Royale*); Sean Connery; George Lazenby and Roger Moore.
SI-2: Bernard Lee (1962–1980), Robert Brown (beginning with *Octopussy*), Edward Fox (*Never Say Never Again*), John Huston (*Casino Royale*).
SI-3: Sean Connery.
SI-4: *Thunderball*.
SI-5: Six.
SI-6: Mr. Waverly.
SI-7: A small device in his wristwatch that re-started his heart—so he would be *In Like Flint*.
SI-8: *Octopussy*.
SI-9: Stephanie Powers.
SI-10: Bond. James Bond.
SI-11: Anthony Zerbe.
SI-12: Mrs. Emma Peel and John Steed.
SI-13: Willie Garvin.
SI-14: Dean Martin (films) and Tony Franciosa (TV).

SI-15: United Network Command for Law Enforcement.
SI-16: Impossible Missions Force.
SI-17: Supreme Headquarters International Espionage Law-Enforcement Division.
SI-18: You would carry a visual scanning device on a ring or a tie clip. And you would have a transmitter and earphone implanted in an ear (TV's *Search*).
SI-19: Would you believe . . . three.
SI-20: *You Only Live Twice* and *Moonraker*.
SI-21: Jack Flack. Dabney Coleman.
SI-22: Hugh O'Brien, Tony Franciosa and Doug McClure.
SI-23: John Steed (Patrick Macnee, *The Avengers*).
SI-24: Your thoughts.
SI-25: *Chitty Chitty Bang Bang*.

THE THING PHOTO: COPYRIGHT © 1982 UNIVERSAL CITY STUDIOS

## Scary Stuff

*(Questions appear on pages 142–43)*
SS-1: 1313 Mockingbird Lane.
SS-2: "The Colour Out of Space."
SS-3: Count Dracula. Chaney—*Son of Dracula* (1943); Niven—*Old Dracula* (1976); Carradine—*House of Frankenstein* (1944), *House of Dracula* (1945) and *Billy the Kid vs. Dracula* (1966).
SS-4: In flames.
SS-5: Elsa Lanchester. She also essayed the title role.
SS-6: Good Lord, it was full of vampires!
SS-7: A hat, an occasional cigar and hair.
SS-8: Veronica Cartwright.
SS-9: The Tasmanian Devil in Warner Brothers cartoon.
SS-10: Michael Jackson (*Thriller*).
SS-11: "Murder" spelled backwards, and what Danny saw in the mirror in *The Shining*.
SS-12: 1957 Chevrolet (book) but a 1958 Plymouth in the film.
SS-13: Fats.
SS-14: Man (from John Carpenter's *The Thing* ad campaign).
SS-15: Bela Lugosi was the monster and Lon Chaney Jr., the Wolf Man. Chaney also put on the monster makeup for a few scenes.

SS-16: *The Munsters*.

SS-17: Wednesday and Pugsley.

SS-18: A bucket of pig's blood drops on her from the rafters of the school gym. It's messy. No wonder she's upset.

SS-19: Lloyd.

SS-20: Mrs. Bates (Norman's alter-ego).

SS-21: "Innsmouth."

SS-22: The Overlook Hotel.

SS-23: *ALIEN*.

SS-24: Jack Pierce.

SS-25: Lon Chaney.

# Legends & Myths

*(Questions appear on pages 144–46)*

LM-1: Merlin's nickname for Arthur, the rightful ruler of all Britain (*The Once and Future King*).

LM-2: "I," said the Sparrow, "with my bow and arrow."

LM-3: *A Connecticut Yankee in King Arthur's Court* (1889).

LM-4: Chuck Yeager.

LM-5: George Pal.

LM-6: *The Seventh Voyage of Sinbad, The Golden Voyage of Sinbad* and *Sinbad and the Eye of the Tiger*. At one time, he was developing a further project—*Sinbad on Mars*.

LM-7: Author Robert Lynn Asprin.

LM-8: Morgan Le Fey.

LM-9: Alfred Bester.

LM-10: *Krull*. (Though their wedding *was* interrupted . . .)

LM-11: Grow up.

LM-12: Richard Wagner.

LM-13: Excalibur.

LM-14: Fritz Lang.

LM-15: *Exorcist II—The Heretic*. It was not a legend, more of a near myth—err, miss.

LM-16: English poet Percy Bysshe Shelley. (Mary Shelley was the author, of course.)

LM-17: Big trouble in the form of a pentagram.

LM-18: You get stoned—i.e. you turn to stone.
LM-19: A pagan fertility cult and human sacrifice. Eventually, he also finds death.
LM-20: Joseph Campbell's *The Hero with a Thousand Faces*.
LM-21: The Lady of the Lake.
LM-22: Buddy Ebsen. He had to quit when he developed an allergy to the silver makeup.
LM-23: "And within strange aeons, even Death may die." (H.P. Lovecraft, the oft-quoted section of *The Necronomicon*).
LM-24: "Space, the final frontier. These are the voyages of the Starship *Enterprise*. Its five-year mission: to explore strange new worlds, to seek out new life and new civilizations, to boldly go where no man has gone before."
LM-25: Gor.

## Tarzans

*(Questions appear on pages 147–49)*
T-1: Kala.
T-2: *Tarzan and the Apes* (1914) and *Tarzan and the Castaways* (1964).
T-3: N'Kima (books) and Cheetah (films).
T-4: Fritz Leiber (*Tarzan and the Valley of Gold*, 1966).
T-5: Elmo Lincoln (1918).
T-6: Christopher Lambert (1984).
T-7: He is *never* called Tarzan in the film, *Greystoke*.
T-8: Boy. Johnny Sheffield.
T-9: Korak the Killer, also Korak, Son of Tarzan. Jack Clayton.
T-10: Burne Hogarth.
T-11: La, Princess of Opar.
T-12: He was the son-in-law of the character's creator, Edgar Rice Burroughs.
T-13: Maureen Sullivan. Director John Farrow. Mia Farrow.
T-14: 13. He made 12 Tarzan films and a 13th appearance in the role, in a cameo in 1943's *Stage Door Canteen*.
T-15: Once. In *Tarzan the Fearless* (1933).

T-16: Jack Benny and Carol Burnett. Burnett did her version of the Tarzan yell.

T-17: The Waziri.

T-18: Jungle Jim.

T-19: Bomba, the Jungle Boy.

T-20: Tarzana (named after Burroughs' character).

T-21: He thought Jane had been killed by Germans and went on a vengeful rampage.

T-22: Jad-Bal-Ja.

T-23: Mark Spitz.

T-24: *Tarzan's Greatest Adventure* (1959). Sean Connery was in it.

T-25: 23 novels, one short story collection, two juvenile Tarzan novels. (There are also an unfinished novel, another short story and a playlet—all unpublished.)

# Truly Bad Sci-Fi

*(Questions appear on pages 150–52)*

TB-1: Dexter Riley (Kurt Russell) got his smarts at Medfield College. While matriculating, he also became *The Strongest Man in the World* and turned invisible in *Now You See Him, Now You Don't*.

TB-2: It mass-produced girl robots clad in gold bikinis, of course.

TB-3: *Plan 9 from Outer Space*. (Of course, this is a matter of opinion, other answers might be acceptable. Consult your conscience.)

TB-4: Michael Landon.

TB-5: *It*!

TB-6: Got real big in *Attack of the 50-Foot Woman*.

TB-7: The planet Porno.

TB-8: *The Ghost in the Invisible Bikini*.

TB-9: For love.

TB-10: Salt water.

TB-11: Pia Zadora. (She was a child at the time.)

TB-12: Jerry Lewis.

TB-13: Albert Dekker.

TB-14: Make people real small (doll size) through his miniaturization technique.

TB-15: *The Green Slime*!
TB-16: The Three Stooges.
TB-17: Adam (Batman) West. (Yes, his character died).
TB-18: A man and a dog.
TB-19: *Galaxina*, Dorothy Stratten.
TB-20: Chuck McCann and Bob Denver.
TB-21: Zsa Zsa Gabor, Dahlink.
TB-22: *Moon*opoly. No, seriously!
TB-23: Ruth Buzzi and Jim Nabors.
TB-24: Ernest Borgnine in *The Black Hole*.
TB-25: *Megaforce*.

## The End of the World

*(Questions appear on pages 153–55)*
EW-1:   U.S. President Merkin Muffey, Group Commander Lionel Mandrake, and the title role.
EW-2:   *When Worlds Collide*. Destination: planet Zyra.
EW-3:   September 13, by thermonuclear explosions.
EW-4:   *Red Alert* by Peter George.
EW-5:   Earth and Bellus.
EW-6:   *I Am Legend*. Price—*The Last Man on Earth* (1964); Heston—*The Omega Man* (1971).
EW-7:   Six nuns and a priest.
EW-8:   Everyone in the world over 25 succumbs to instant old age from nerve gas.
EW-9:   Krypton, Alderaan, Earth and Squootpeep.
EW-10:  Stops the Earth on its axis, creating a great hurricane.
EW-11:  Captain ''King'' Kong (played by Slim Pickens).
EW-12:  Moscow and New York.
EW-13:  The Environmental Protection Agency (EPA).
EW-14:  To make way for an Intergalactic By-Pass.
EW-15:  Australia.
EW-16:  California.
EW-17:  The entire population of the Soviet Union.
EW-18:  Harry Belafonte, Mel Ferrer and Inger Stevens.
EW-19:  New York City.
EW-20:  Lawrence, Kansas. (This, too, could be *your* town.)
EW-21:  Robots and dogs.

EW-22: The Humungus.

EW-23: Plague.

EW-24: Plague again, caused by a germ warfare research accident.

EW-25: They turned to dust.

## Photo Answers

Page 9: Dick Miller and Robby the Robot.

Page 11: Truck driver (and adventurer!) Russell and Carpenter have teamed four times: *Elvis*, *Escape from New York*, *The Thing*, and *Big Trouble in Little China*.

Page 14: *Love of Life*.

Page 15: *Cutter's Goose*.

Page 16: "Chim Chim Cheree."

Page 20: Adam Link.

Page 22: *The Valley of Gwangi*.

Page 25: "Ship, out of danger?"

Page 28: Charles Middleton.

Page 29: David Prowse.

Page 33: The one on the right (Leonard Nimoy).

Page 35: 167 minutes (some prints are shorter).

Page 42: They are both Kirk ("The Enemy Within").

Page 44: "There is Nothing Like a Dame."

Page 47: Eddie Quint, the werewolf of Joe Dante's *The Howling*. Picardo was also Meg Mucklebones, devised by Bottin, for Ridley Scott's *Legend*.

Page 51: Electric batteries and Twinkies.

Page 55: *Wizards and Warriors*.

Page 59: Leia (Ann Sachs), C-3PO (Anthony Daniels), Han Solo (Perry King).

Page 67: Maurice Evans. Kim Hunter.

Page 69: *Poltergeist*. Heather O'Rourke.

Page 70: Leela (Louise Jameson).

Page 73: Tom Baker (in the rear). He's a waxwork.

Page 74: The Three Stooges (*in Orbit*).

Page 78: Patrick Macnee.

Page 80: Four (sound, sound editing, visual effects, original score).

Page 87: Edgar Wallace.
Page 90: William Shakespeare, "The Bard."
Page 93: Herman Melville's *Moby Dick*.
Page 96: Cole Porter. "Anything Goes."
Page 100: Chuck Jones.
Page 101: The shaving cream atom, you silly wabbit.
Page 103: *Duel* (It's Steven Spielberg).
Page 106: They were the same race until they were split by the crystal and became separate entities.
Page 112: Andrea McArdle.
Page 113: Kirk Alyn. Superman.
Page 114: He's the son of Bill Keane, of *The Family Circus*.
Page 117: Michael Ironside.
Page 119: On his trip to Mars.
Page 122: George Pal.
Page 125: Jon-Erik Hexum, Meeno Peluce: *Voyagers* (and actors). Arthur C. Clarke (author).
Page 128: *Metropolis*.
Page 131: *The Vulture*.
Page 133: Just Another F***ing Observer.
Page 136: Nuclear holocaust.
Page 139: Rock 'n' roll.
Page 145: Human.
Page 149: 1932.
Page 151: Barry Bostwick, Persis Khambatta (*Megaforce*).
Page 155: Tim McIntire.